I0620688

DANTE'S PURGATORIO

By DANTE ALIGHIERI

Translated by
HENRY WADSWORTH LONGFELLOW

Introduction by
WILLIAM WARREN VERNON

Dante's Purgatorio (The Divine Comedy: Volume II, Purgatory)
By Dante Alighieri
Translated by Henry Wadsworth Longfellow
Introduction by William Warren Vernon

Print ISBN 13: 978-1-4209-7462-1
eBook ISBN 13: 978-1-4209-7629-8

This edition copyright © 2021. Digireads.com Publishing.

All rights reserved. No part of this publication may be reproduced, distributed, or transmitted in any form or by any means, including photocopying, recording, or other electronic or mechanical methods, without the prior written permission of the publisher, except in the case of brief quotations embodied in critical reviews and certain other noncommercial uses permitted by copyright law.

Cover Image: "La Divina Commedia di Dante" (Dante and the Divine Comedy) by Domenico di Michelino. c. 1465 fresco, in the dome of the church of Santa Maria del Fiore in Florence.

Please visit *www.digireads.com*

CONTENTS

PURGATORIO

Introduction

I. DESCRIPTION OF PURGATORY.

The Mountain of Purgatory, as described by Dante, is an immense truncated cone, rising out of the midst of the sea in the centre of the Southern Hemisphere, which, according to the Ptolemaic system of Cosmography, consisted, with the exception of the mountain in question, of a vast ocean. Purgatory is supposed to be situated at the exact antipodes to Jerusalem, and to have been formed by the fall of Lucifer, which in Readings on the Inferno (2nd ed., vol. ii, pp. 656, 657), is thus described:—

"In the headlong velocity with which Lucifer was hurled down from the highest Heaven (the Empyrean), weighed by the load of his immense sin, he struck the earth with such force, as to pierce through the bowels of it; nor was his downward course arrested, until the occult forces that were erroneously supposed to exist in the centre of the earth bound him there. The earth, recoiling in horror at the sight and at the contact of so abominable a monster, then went through two operations, the first to avoid the sight of him, and the second to avoid the contact of him.

"(*a*) To avoid the sight of him, it sought to cover itself with the waters on that side where he fell; and to hollow out a bed for the waters, it set in motion mountains, hills, islands, etc., which fled from thence and came up to our hemisphere; whereupon the oceans, which had up till then been in our hemisphere rushed furiously into the Southern Hemisphere to fill up the void. And by this operation it came about that the Northern Hemisphere now consists of elevated and inhabited continents, while the other [according to the Cosmography of those times] is filled up by the great Ocean, and is without a single inhabitant.

"(*b*) To avoid touching him, the inner bowels of the earth, through which the fallen monster passed, seized with terror and disgust, all rushed upwards; and these masses, heaping themselves one upon another on that side where was the Earthly Paradise which alone had not moved, rose to form the island-mountain of Purgatory," leaving behind them the cavernous opening through which Dante and Virgil wound their way upwards when they quitted Hell.

Let us bear in mind that Dante supposes our first parents to have lived in innocence in the beautiful region on the top of the Mountain of Purgatory. When, in consequence of their sin, they were driven forth from Paradise, they had to take up their abode in the Northern Hemisphere. The Mountain of Purgatory is described as having three principal divisions: Ante-Purgatory, Purgatory Proper, and Post-

Purgatory, usually called the Terrestrial Paradise.

Ante-Purgatory is the lower region at the foot of the mountain, in which are found the spirits of those who from indolence delayed repentance, or died in contumacy of Holy Church, and are doomed, as Manfred tells Dante (Canto iii, 136-141), to remain outside the gate of Purgatory for a period of thirty times the length of the time that they delayed their repentance, unless the term were shortened in answer to the prayers of virtuous persons on earth. It will be noticed throughout this *Cantica* with what earnestness nearly all the spirits that Dante meets beseech his kind intervention with their relations, to urge them to dedicate prayers for the acceleration of their passage through Purgatory. Even in Paradise, Cacciaguida tells Dante that his son, Dante's great-grandfather, has been for a hundred years encircling the Cornice where pride is punished, and that Dante ought to shorten his prolonged sufferings by his good offices on behalf of his ancestor.

> "Ben si convien che la lunga fatica
> Tu gli raccorci con T opere tue."—Par. xv, 95, 96.

Ante-Purgatory is described in the first eight Cantos. In Canto ix Dante falls into a deep sleep, and is carried by an eagle to the gate of Purgatory, into which he is admitted by an Angel, who, with his sword, inscribes upon his brow seven P's representing the seven deadly sins, which will have to be erased in succession, as each is purged in its corresponding Cornice.

Purgatory Proper.—Within the gates are the seven Cornices or terraces just mentioned, each being in width about three times the length of a man's body. These Cornices run right round the mountain, and, at the end of each, a hollow stairway, cut out of the solid rock, leads straight up to the next Cornice. At the entrance to each stairway stands the Angel of the Cornice, who, before permitting the penitent to quit it, effaces with the point of his shining wing, the P (out of the seven marked on his brow) which denotes the sin that has been purged away in that Cornice. Whenever the pilgrims reach the summit of a stairway, they turn to the right, whereas, on entering the circles of Hell, they nearly always had turned to the left. Another peculiarity to be noticed in Purgatory is that, when night falls, they must perforce delay their further progress until the sunrise of the ensuing day. We learn too from Canto xxi, 70, that, whenever a soul has completed its penance and purification, the mountain thrills with joy, and all the other souls burst out into a *Gloria in Excelsis.* Above the level of the gate of Purgatory all atmospheric influences, such as rain, wind, hail, snow, frost, etc., entirely cease. Higher up, in the Terrestial Paradise, there is indeed a wind which moves the leaves of the forest, but that is supposed to be produced by the rapid movement of the Sphere of

Heaven, denominated the *Primum Mobile.*

The Terrestrial Paradise, or Post-Purgatory.—The penitents who have gone through all the seven Cornices, when they leave the last one, have to pass through the purifying fire, and then ascend by a lofty stair to the summit of the mountain. They here find themselves in the ancient Garden of Eden, the Terrestrial Paradise, which, lovely and deserted, has remained in its pristine beauty since the expulsion of our first parents, with its luxuriant herbage, with its spreading trees, whose leaves are gently moved by a warm and perfumed air, with its flowers of many colors, and with its warbling birds.

The wind and the water of two streams, Lethe and Eunoe, which flow through the Terrestrial Paradise in opposite directions, are produced from supernatural sources, the first-named river being endued with power to take away the memory of sin, but only of sin; the other, to call every virtuous deed to mind.

II. TIME OCCUPIED IN PASSING THROUGH PURGATORY, AND SUPPOSED DATE OF THE VISION.

Dr. Moore (*Time References,* p. 3 *et seq.*), observes that the date 1300 has been all but universally accepted, from the time of the earliest Commentators down to the present day. There are four passages which strongly support this argument.

First.—In the opening line of the *Inferno,* Dante speaks of himself as being half-way through the path-way of his life. In the *Convivio*[1] (iv, 23, 11. 88-110), he states definitely that human life is like an arch, whose highest point is thirty-five years; and for this reason it was the will of Christ to die in His thirty-fourth year, for it was not fitting that the Deity should abide in such decay (*stare in discrescere*).[2] Dante then has interpreted the first line of the *Inferno* as meaning that he was thirty-five years old, and, as he was born in the year 1265, he would consequently be of that age in the year 1300.

Second.—Guido Cavalcanti is known to have died on the 27th or 28th August, 1300. In *Inferno,* x, 110, 111, Dante informs Guido's father that he was alive.

Third.—In *Purgatorio.* ii, 98, Casella tells Dante that the Indulgence, connected with the Jubilee of Boniface VIII, began just three months before, and that he and other spirits, delayed at the mouth of the Tiber, had felt the benefit of it. This Indulgence was proclaimed

---

[1] In the third edition of the Oxford Test (1904) Dr. Moore has substituted the titles "*Convivio*" for "*Convito*," and "*De Vulgari Eloquentia*" for "*De Vulgari Eloquio.*" Henceforth I shall make use of the same terms.

[2] It would of course be Christ's *Humanity* which would decrease after His thirty-fifth year, not His Divinity. And what Dante means is that it was not fitting that the Godhead should abide in decaying Manhood.

on the 22nd February, 1300, but its privileges were antedated in the Bull itself from the Christmas Day preceding. This, as Dr. Moore points out, necessitates the spring of 1300.

Finally, Dante relates all events that had happened before 1300 as past, but speaks prophetically of all that occurred after 1300 as future events.

Throughout the *Purgatorio* Dante gives continual indications of time, and we are thus able to trace his progress far more closely than in the *Inferno*, which he took twenty-five hours to traverse.

He is four days going through Purgatory.

In Ante-Purgatory one day, Easter Day (Canto i, 19, to Canto ix, 9).

In Purgatory proper two days, namely, Easter Monday (Canto ix, 13, to Canto xviii, 76), and Easter Tuesday (Canto xix, 1, to Canto xxvii, 89).

In the Terrestrial Paradise one day, Easter Wednesday (Canto xxvii, 94, to Canto xxxiii, 103).

Although there is much dispute as to the day of the week, or month, on which the journey through Purgatory is supposed to take place, and also as to some of the hours indicated on several days, there is no doubt about the aggregate of time allowed.

There are as many as thirty definite references to time. The last is in Canto xxxiii, 103, and refers to the hour of noon on Easter Wednesday, 13th April, 1300.

III. THE PRINCIPAL DIVISIONS OF THE PURGATORIO.

Ante-Purgatory is described in Cantos i to ix.

Purgatory proper in Cantos ix to xxviii.

The Terrestrial Paradise, or Post-Purgatory, in Cantos xxviii to xxxiii. At the end of the last Canto of the Purgatorio Dante says:—

> "piene son tutte le carte
> Ordite a questa Cantica seconda."

In the divisions of his poem Dante scrupulously observes the rules of symmetry. Each of the three Cantiche has thirty-three Cantos, inasmuch as the first Canto of the *Inferno* must be considered as the Introduction or Preface to the whole poem. And in fact, in the *Inferno*, the Invocation is not in the first Canto, as it is in the *Purgatorio* and *Paradiso*, but in the second.

The hundred Cantos of the *Divina Commedia* consist of 14,233 verses, of which

The *Inferno* has 4,720 verses.
The *Purgatorio* 4,755 verses.
The *Paradiso* 4,758 verses.

A parallel case is noted by Professor Charles Eliot Norton, as regards the poems in the *Vita Nuova*, which Dante has constructed with the most perfect symmetry, namely: 10 Minor poems, 1 Canzone, 4 Minor poems, 1 Canzone, 4 Minor poems, 1 Canzone, 10 Minor poems.

IV. DATE WHEN THE PURGATORIO WAS WRITTEN.

There is every reason to suppose that the *Purgatorio* was written before the end of 1314. Philip *le Bel*, King of France, died 29th November, 1314, and is referred to as still living in the last Canto (xxxiii, 34).

"Sappi che il vaso che il serpente ruppe,
    Fu, e non è; ma chi n' ha colpa, creda
    Che vendetta di Dio non teme suppe."

This passage, which is intended to censure Clement V and *Philip le Bel* for having transferred the Papal Throne to Avignon, would seem to show that Philip was not dead when these lines were written, and, as they occur in the last Canto of the *Purgatorio*, that Division of the *Divina Commedia* must have been written previously to November, 1314.

In the twenty-fourth Canto an allusion is made to Dante falling in love with Gentucca at Lucca, which we know cannot have happened earlier than 1314, as it was only on the 14th June, 1314, that Uguccione della Faggiuola made himself master of Lucca, which city, up to that time, had been bitterly hostile to Henry VII, as well as to the Ghibellines and the *Bianchi*. The twenty-fourth Canto, in which Lucca is mentioned, could not have been written *earlier* than June, 1314, and the thirty-third or last Canto could not have been written *later* than November, 1314. Thus within six months Dante must have written at least ten Cantos. The invectives against the Emperor Albert, in the Sixth Canto, appear to have been written before his successor visited Italy in 1310. It would seem therefore that the composition of the *Purgatorio* must have occupied five years, from 1310 to 1314, or even six years. Cesare Balbo thinks it probable that Dante began it in 1309, during his quiet residence in Paris, that he continued it in 1310 amid his first hopes of Henry's visit, and then paused; that he resumed it with fresh vigour after that Emperor's death, and finished it during the last months of 1314. Witte (*Dante-Forschungen*) does not think that the *Purgatorio* was finished before 1319. Dean Plumptre is of opinion that the *Purgatorio* was the most rapidly written of all the three parts of the *Divina Commedia*, and that the period of its composition embraced the years 1308-12, in which Dante was watching with hope the election of Henry VII to the Imperial Throne, and the preparations for the Italian expedition.

V. NATURE OF THE PURGATORIO AS COMPARED WITH THE INFERNO.

Cesare Balbo says "the *Purgatorio*, taking it altogether, is perhaps the most beautiful part of the *Divina Commedia*, or that at least which exemplifies the best, the most beautiful part of Dante's character, his love." After passing through the *Inferno*, "Dante had now issued from the gloom of the infernal abyss, into the light, and Sun, and hopes of Purgatory; in his real existence he had abandoned the thoughts of his ungrateful country and her factions, and was cherishing hopes of peace and repose, as is natural to an exile treading a foreign land."

In the *Inferno* all is gloom and darkness; the indications of the time of day are invariably given by allusions to the position of the Moon; the Sun is never alluded to from the moment when Dante has passed within the gates of Hell, until the point when, after the Poets have passed the centre of the Earth, and are about to commence the ascent of the Southern Hemisphere, Virgil indicates the hour to Dante by a reference to the Sun:—

"E già il sole a mezza terza riede."—*Inf.* xxxiv, 96.

As soon as Purgatory is entered, Dante makes us feel the Sun's actual presence.

While out of a whole so harmonious and perfect it is difficult to select passages in the *Purgatorio* for marked preference, we may nevertheless dwell upon a few of unsurpassed excellence. These are: The description of the four bright stars and the sweet colour of Oriental sapphire in Canto i; the sunrise, and the approach of the Angel in the vessel which he propels by his wings, and the singing of Casella in Canto ii; the conversations with Manfred in Canto iii; Belacqua in Canto iv; Buonconte da Montefeltro, and Pia de Tolomei in Canto v; the outburst of indignation against the feuds and factions of Italy in Canto vi; the night in the Flowery Valley, and the souls of the great in Canto vii; the Compline Hymn, Nino Visconti di Gallura, the serpent driven away by the Angels, and the noble words that pass between Dante and Conrad Malaspina in Canto viii; the Gate of Purgatory, and Dante's admittance within it in Canto ix; the sculptures and Trajan in

Canto x; the Lord's Prayer and Oderisi d' Agobbio the miniature painter, in Canto xi; Sapía of Siena in Canto xiii; Guido del Duca's invective against the cities of Tuscany in Canto xiv; the conversation with Marco Lombardo in Canto xvi; the interviews with Adrian V, the good Pope, in Canto xix; and with Hugh Capet in Canto xx; the appearance of Statius in Canto xxi; the description by Statius of the early Christians in Canto xxii; Forese Donati in Canto xxiii; then the beautiful picture of the Terrestrial Paradise and the appearance of Matelda in Cantos xxvii and xxviii; and last of all, the three allegorical Cantos, xxix, xxx and xxxi, when Dante again meets Beatrice after a lapse, according to the fiction, of ten years, but in reality of twenty-four years since her death.

Another peculiar feature in the *Purgatorio*, as in contrast to the *Inferno*, is the numerous appearances of Angels. There is only one Angel mentioned in Hell, he who came down to open the gates of the City of Dis, but even the identity of this personage with one of the Angels of God is, wrongly, I think, disputed. In the *Purgatorio*, however, Angels are continually encountered, and on the appearance of the first one Virgil says to Dante:—

"Omai vedrai di si fatti offiziali."—*Purg.* ii, 30.

The Purgatorio closes with a prophecy by Beatrice of the advent of a mysterious personage, whom she styles the "Five hundred, ten, and five." This is usually interpreted to denote the three letters "D.X.V.," which when inverted form the word "DVX," "Leader," and evidently means some great Ghibelline Captain of the time. Recent research points almost conclusively to the Emperor Henry VII, as the personage indicated. See Dr. Moore, *Studies*, iii, in the article on "The DXV Prophecy," pp. 253-283. Also see *The Pilot* of April, 1901, article on "Dante's Prophetical Enigma—A New Solution," by D. R. Fearon, C.B.

WILLIAM WARREN VERNON

Readings on the Purgatorio of Dante, "Preliminary Chapter," 1889.

Purgatorio

Canto I

To run o'er better waters hoists its sail
  The little vessel of my genius now,
  That leaves behind itself a sea so cruel;

And of that second kingdom will I sing
  Wherein the human spirit doth purge itself,
  And to ascend to heaven becometh worthy.

But let dead Poesy here rise again,
  O holy Muses, since that I am yours,
  And here Calliope somewhat ascend,

My song accompanying with that sound,
  Of which the miserable magpies felt
  The blow so great, that they despaired of pardon.

Sweet color of the oriental sapphire,
  That was upgathered in the cloudless aspect
  Of the pure air, as far as the first circle,

Unto mine eyes did recommence delight
  Soon as I issued forth from the dead air,
  Which had with sadness filled mine eyes and breast.

The beauteous planet, that to love incites,
  Was making all the orient to laugh,
  Veiling the Fishes that were in her escort.

To the right hand I turned, and fixed my mind
  Upon the other pole, and saw four stars
  Ne'er seen before save by the primal people.

Rejoicing in their flamelets seemed the heaven.
  O thou septentrional and widowed site,
  Because thou art deprived of seeing these!

When from regarding them I had withdrawn,
  Turning a little to the other pole,
  There where the Wain had disappeared already,

I saw beside me an old man alone,
  Worthy of so much reverence in his look,
  That more owes not to father any son.

A long beard and with white hair intermingled
  He wore, in semblance like unto the tresses,
  Of which a double list fell on his breast.

The rays of the four consecrated stars
  Did so adorn his countenance with light,
  That him I saw as were the sun before him.

"Who are you? ye who, counter the blind river,
  Have fled away from the eternal prison?"
  Moving those venerable plumes, he said:

"Who guided you? or who has been your lamp
  In issuing forth out of the night profound,
  That ever black makes the infernal valley?

The laws of the abyss, are they thus broken?
  Or is there changed in heaven some council new,
  That being damned ye come unto my crags?"

Then did my Leader lay his grasp upon me,
  And with his words, and with his hands and signs,
  Reverent he made in me my knees and brow;

Then answered him: "I came not of myself;
  A Lady from Heaven descended, at whose prayers
  I aided this one with my company.

But since it is thy will more be unfolded
  Of our condition, how it truly is,
  Mine cannot be that this should be denied thee.

This one has never his last evening seen,
  But by his folly was so near to it
  That very little time was there to turn.

As I have said, I unto him was sent
  To rescue him, and other way was none
  Than this to which I have myself betaken.

I've shown him all the people of perdition,
  And now those spirits I intend to show
  Who purge themselves beneath thy guardianship.

How I have brought him would be long to tell thee.
  Virtue descendeth from on high that aids me
  To lead him to behold thee and to hear thee.

Now may it please thee to vouchsafe his coming;
  He seeketh Liberty, which is so dear,
  As knoweth he who life for her refuses.

Thou know'st it; since, for her, to thee not bitter
  Was death in Utica, where thou didst leave
  The vesture, that will shine so, the great day.

By us the eternal edicts are not broken;
  Since this one lives, and Minos binds not me;
  But of that circle I, where are the chaste

Eyes of thy Marcia, who in looks still prays thee,
  O holy breast, to hold her as thine own;
  For her love, then, incline thyself to us.

Permit us through thy sevenfold realm to go;
  I will take back this grace from thee to her,
  If to be mentioned there below thou deignest."

"Marcia so pleasing was unto mine eyes
  While I was on the other side," then said he,
  "That every grace she wished of me I granted;

Now that she dwells beyond the evil river,
  She can no longer move me, by that law
  Which, when I issued forth from there, was made.

But if a Lady of Heaven do move and rule thee,
  As thou dost say, no flattery is needful;
  Let it suffice thee that for her thou ask me.

Go, then, and see thou gird this one about
  With a smooth rush, and that thou wash his face,
  So that thou cleanse away all stain therefrom,

For 'twere not fitting that the eye o'ercast
  By any mist should go before the first
  Angel, who is of those of Paradise.

This little island round about its base
  Below there, yonder, where the billow beats it,
  Doth rushes bear upon its washy ooze;

No other plant that putteth forth the leaf,
  Or that doth indurate, can there have life,
  Because it yieldeth not unto the shocks.

Thereafter be not this way your return;
  The sun, which now is rising, will direct you
  To take the mount by easier ascent."

With this he vanished; and I raised me up
  Without a word, and wholly drew myself
  Unto my Guide, and turned mine eyes to him.

And he began: "Son, follow thou my steps;
  Let us turn back, for on this side declines
  The plain unto its lower boundaries."

The dawn was vanquishing the matin hour
  Which fled before it, so that from afar
  I recognized the trembling of the sea.

Along the solitary plain we went
  As one who unto the lost road returns,
  And till he finds it seems to go in vain.

As soon as we were come to where the dew
  Fights with the sun, and, being in a part
  Where shadow falls, little evaporates,

Both of his hands upon the grass outspread
  In gentle manner did my Master place;
  Whence I, who of his action was aware,

Extended unto him my tearful cheeks;
  There did he make in me uncovered wholly
  That hue which Hell had covered up in me.

Then came we down upon the desert shore
  Which never yet saw navigate its waters
  Any that afterward had known return.

There he begirt me as the other pleased;
  O marvellous! for even as he culled
  The humble plant, such it sprang up again

Suddenly there where he uprooted it.

Canto II

Already had the sun the horizon reached
  Whose circle of meridian covers o'er
  Jerusalem with its most lofty point,

And night that opposite to him revolves
  Was issuing forth from Ganges with the Scales
  That fall from out her hand when she exceedeth;

So that the white and the vermilion cheeks
  Of beautiful Aurora, where I was,
  By too great age were changing into orange.

We still were on the border of the sea,
  Like people who are thinking of their road,
  Who go in heart and with the body stay;

And lo! as when, upon the approach of morning,
  Through the gross vapours Mars grows fiery red
  Down in the West upon the ocean floor,

Appeared to me—may I again behold it!—
  A light along the sea so swiftly coming,
  Its motion by no flight of wing is equalled;

From which when I a little had withdrawn
  Mine eyes, that I might question my Conductor,
  Again I saw it brighter grown and larger.

Then on each side of it appeared to me
  I knew not what of white, and underneath it
  Little by little there came forth another.

My Master yet had uttered not a word
  While the first whiteness into wings unfolded;
  But when he clearly recognized the pilot,

He cried: "Make haste, make haste to bow the knee!
  Behold the Angel of God! fold thou thy hands!
  Henceforward shalt thou see such officers!

See how he scorneth human arguments,
  So that nor oar he wants, nor other sail
  Than his own wings, between so distant shores.

See how he holds them pointed up to heaven,
  Fanning the air with the eternal pinions,
  That do not moult themselves like mortal hair!"

Then as still nearer and more near us came
  The Bird Divine, more radiant he appeared,
  So that near by the eye could not endure him,

But down I cast it; and he came to shore
  With a small vessel, very swift and light,
  So that the water swallowed naught thereof.

Upon the stern stood the Celestial Pilot;
  Beatitude seemed written in his face,
  And more than a hundred spirits sat within.

"In exitu Israel de Aegypto!"
  They chanted all together in one voice,
  With whatso in that psalm is after written.

Then made he sign of holy rood upon them,
  Whereat all cast themselves upon the shore,
  And he departed swiftly as he came.

The throng which still remained there unfamiliar
  Seemed with the place, all round about them gazing,
  As one who in new matters makes essay.

On every side was darting forth the day.
  The sun, who had with his resplendent shafts
  From the mid-heaven chased forth the Capricorn,

When the new people lifted up their faces
  Towards us, saying to us: "If ye know,
  Show us the way to go unto the mountain."

And answer made Virgilius: "Ye believe
  Perchance that we have knowledge of this place,
  But we are strangers even as yourselves.

Just now we came, a little while before you,
  Another way, which was so rough and steep,
  That mounting will henceforth seem sport to us."

The souls who had, from seeing me draw breath,
  Become aware that I was still alive,
  Pallid in their astonishment became;

And as to messenger who bears the olive
  The people throng to listen to the news,
  And no one shows himself afraid of crowding,

So at the sight of me stood motionless
  Those fortunate spirits, all of them, as if
  Oblivious to go and make them fair.

One from among them saw I coming forward,
  As to embrace me, with such great affection,
  That it incited me to do the like.

O empty shadows, save in aspect only!
  Three times behind it did I clasp my hands,
  As oft returned with them to my own breast!

I think with wonder I depicted me;
  Whereat the shadow smiled and backward drew;
  And I, pursuing it, pressed farther forward.

Gently it said that I should stay my steps;
  Then knew I who it was, and I entreated
  That it would stop awhile to speak with me.

It made reply to me: "Even as I loved thee
  In mortal body, so I love thee free;
  Therefore I stop; but wherefore goest thou?"

"My own Casella! to return once more
   There where I am, I make this journey," said I;
   "But how from thee has so much time be taken?"

And he to me: "No outrage has been done me,
   If he who takes both when and whom he pleases
   Has many times denied to me this passage,

For of a righteous will his own is made.
   He, sooth to say, for three months past has taken
   Whoever wished to enter with all peace;

Whence I, who now had turned unto that shore
   Where salt the waters of the Tiber grow,
   Benignantly by him have been received.

Unto that outlet now his wing is pointed,
   Because for evermore assemble there
   Those who tow'rds Acheron do not descend."

And I: "If some new law take not from thee
   Memory or practice of the song of love,
   Which used to quiet in me all my longings,

Thee may it please to comfort therewithal
   Somewhat this soul of mine, that with its body
   Hitherward coming is so much distressed."

"Love, that within my mind discourses with me,"
   Forthwith began he so melodiously,
   The melody within me still is sounding.

My Master, and myself, and all that people
   Which with him were, appeared as satisfied
   As if naught else might touch the mind of any.

We all of us were moveless and attentive
   Unto his notes; and lo! the grave old man,
   Exclaiming: "What is this, ye laggard spirits?

What negligence, what standing still is this?
   Run to the mountain to strip off the slough,
   That lets not God be manifest to you."

Even as when, collecting grain or tares,
  The doves, together at their pasture met,
  Quiet, nor showing their accustomed pride,

If aught appear of which they are afraid,
  Upon a sudden leave their food alone,
  Because they are assailed by greater care;

So that fresh company did I behold
  The song relinquish, and go tow'rds the hill,
  As one who goes, and knows not whitherward;

Nor was our own departure less in haste.

Canto III

Inasmuch as the instantaneous flight
  Had scattered them asunder o'er the plain,
  Turned to the mountain whither reason spurs us,

I pressed me close unto my faithful comrade,
  And how without him had I kept my course?
  Who would have led me up along the mountain?

He seemed to me within himself remorseful;
  O noble conscience, and without a stain,
  How sharp a sting is trivial fault to thee!

After his feet had laid aside the haste
  Which mars the dignity of every act,
  My mind, that hitherto had been restrained,

Let loose its faculties as if delighted,
  And I my sight directed to the hill
  That highest tow'rds the heaven uplifts itself.

The sun, that in our rear was flaming red,
  Was broken in front of me into the figure
  Which had in me the stoppage of its rays;

Unto one side I turned me, with the fear
  Of being left alone, when I beheld
  Only in front of me the ground obscured.

"Why dost thou still mistrust?" my Comforter
  Began to say to me turned wholly round;
  "Dost thou not think me with thee, and that I guide thee?

'Tis evening there already where is buried
  The body within which I cast a shadow;
  'Tis from Brundusium ta'en, and Naples has it.

Now if in front of me no shadow fall,
  Marvel not at it more than at the heavens,
  Because one ray impedeth not another

To suffer torments, both of cold and heat,
  Bodies like this that Power provides, which wills
  That how it works be not unveiled to us.

Insane is he who hopeth that our reason
  Can traverse the illimitable way,
  Which the one Substance in three Persons follows!

Mortals, remain contented at the 'Quia;'
  For if ye had been able to see all,
  No need there were for Mary to give birth;

And ye have seen desiring without fruit,
  Those whose desire would have been quieted,
  Which evermore is given them for a grief.

I speak of Aristotle and of Plato,
  And many others;"—and here bowed his head,
  And more he said not, and remained disturbed.

We came meanwhile unto the mountain's foot;
  There so precipitate we found the rock,
  That nimble legs would there have been in vain.

'Twixt Lerici and Turbia, the most desert,
  The most secluded pathway is a stair
  Easy and open, if compared with that.

"Who knoweth now upon which hand the hill
  Slopes down," my Master said, his footsteps staying,
  "So that who goeth without wings may mount?"

And while he held his eyes upon the ground
  Examining the nature of the path,
  And I was looking up around the rock,

On the left hand appeared to me a throng
  Of souls, that moved their feet in our direction,
  And did not seem to move, they came so slowly.

"Lift up thine eyes," I to the Master said;
  "Behold, on this side, who will give us counsel,
  If thou of thine own self can have it not."

Then he looked at me, and with frank expression
  Replied: "Let us go there, for they come slowly,
  And thou be steadfast in thy hope, sweet son."

Still was that people as far off from us,
  After a thousand steps of ours I say,
  As a good thrower with his hand would reach,

When they all crowded unto the hard masses
  Of the high bank, and motionless stood and close,
  As he stands still to look who goes in doubt.

"O happy dead! O spirits elect already!"
  Virgilius made beginning, "by that peace
  Which I believe is waiting for you all,

Tell us upon what side the mountain slopes,
  So that the going up be possible,
  For to lose time irks him most who most knows."

As sheep come issuing forth from out the fold
  By ones and twos and threes, and the others stand
  Timidly, holding down their eyes and nostrils,

And what the foremost does the others do,
  Huddling themselves against her, if she stop,
  Simple and quiet and the wherefore know not;

So moving to approach us thereupon
  I saw the leader of that fortunate flock,
  Modest in face and dignified in gait.

As soon as those in the advance saw broken
  The light upon the ground at my right side,
  So that from me the shadow reached the rock,

They stopped, and backward drew themselves somewhat;
  And all the others, who came after them,
  Not knowing why nor wherefore, did the same.

"Without your asking, I confess to you
  This is a human body which you see,
  Whereby the sunshine on the ground is cleft.

Marvel ye not thereat, but be persuaded
  That not without a power which comes from Heaven
  Doth he endeavour to surmount this wall."

The Master thus; and said those worthy people:
  "Return ye then, and enter in before us,"
  Making a signal with the back o' the hand

And one of them began: "Whoe'er thou art,
  Thus going turn thine eyes, consider well
  If e'er thou saw me in the other world."

I turned me tow'rds him, and looked at him closely;
  Blond was he, beautiful, and of noble aspect,
  But one of his eyebrows had a blow divided.

When with humility I had disclaimed
  E'er having seen him, "Now behold!" he said,
  And showed me high upon his breast a wound.

Then said he with a smile: "I am Manfredi,
  The grandson of the Empress Costanza;
  Therefore, when thou returnest, I beseech thee

Go to my daughter beautiful, the mother
  Of Sicily's honor and of Aragon's,
  And the truth tell her, if aught else be told.

After I had my body lacerated
  By these two mortal stabs, I gave myself
  Weeping to Him, who willingly doth pardon.

Horrible my iniquities had been;
  But Infinite Goodness hath such ample arms,
  That it receives whatever turns to it.

Had but Cosenza's pastor, who in chase
  Of me was sent by Clement at that time,
  In God read understandingly this page,

The bones of my dead body still would be
  At the bridge-head, near unto Benevento,
  Under the safeguard of the heavy cairn.

Now the rain bathes and moveth them the wind,
  Beyond the realm, almost beside the Verde,
  Where he transported them with tapers quenched.

By malison of theirs is not so lost
  Eternal Love, that it cannot return,
  So long as hope has anything of green.

True is it, who in contumacy dies
  Of Holy Church, though penitent at last,
  Must wait upon the outside this bank

Thirty times told the time that he has been
  In his presumption, unless such decree
  Shorter by means of righteous prayers become.

See now if thou hast power to make me happy,
  By making known unto my good Costanza
  How thou hast seen me, and this ban beside,

For those on earth can much advance us here."

Canto IV

Whenever by delight or else by pain,
  That seizes any faculty of ours,
  Wholly to that the soul collects itself,

It seemeth that no other power it heeds;
  And this against that error is which thinks
  One soul above another kindles in us.

And hence, whenever aught is heard or seen
  Which keeps the soul intently bent upon it,
  Time passes on, and we perceive it not,

Because one faculty is that which listens,
  And other that which the soul keeps entire;
  This is as if in bonds, and that is free.

Of this I had experience positive
  In hearing and in gazing at that spirit;
  For fifty full degrees uprisen was

The sun, and I had not perceived it, when
  We came to where those souls with one accord
  Cried out unto us: "Here is what you ask."

A greater opening ofttimes hedges up
  With but a little forkful of his thorns
  The villager, what time the grape imbrowns,

Than was the passage-way through which ascended
  Only my Leader and myself behind him,
  After that company departed from us.

One climbs Sanleo and descends in Noli,
  And mounts the summit of Bismantova,
  With feet alone; but here one needs must fly;

With the swift pinions and the plumes I say
  Of great desire, conducted after him
  Who gave me hope, and made a light for me.

We mounted upward through the rifted rock,
  And on each side the border pressed upon us,
  And feet and hands the ground beneath required.

When we were come upon the upper rim
  Of the high bank, out on the open slope,
  "My Master," said I, "what way shall we take?"

And he to me: "No step of thine descend;
  Still up the mount behind me win thy way,
  Till some sage escort shall appear to us."

The summit was so high it vanquished sight,
  And the hillside precipitous far more
  Than line from middle quadrant to the centre.

Spent with fatigue was I, when I began:
  "O my sweet Father! turn thee and behold
  How I remain alone, unless thou stay!"

"O son," he said, "up yonder drag thyself,"
  Pointing me to a terrace somewhat higher,
  Which on that side encircles all the hill.

These words of his so spurred me on, that I
  Strained every nerve, behind him scrambling up,
  Until the circle was beneath my feet.

Thereon ourselves we seated both of us
  Turned to the East, from which we had ascended,
  For all men are delighted to look back.

To the low shores mine eyes I first directed,
  Then to the sun uplifted them, and wondered
  That on the left hand we were smitten by it.

The Poet well perceived that I was wholly
  Bewildered at the chariot of the light,
  Where 'twixt us and the Aquilon it entered.

Whereon he said to me: "If Castor and Pollux
  Were in the company of yonder mirror,
  That up and down conducteth with its light,

Thou wouldst behold the zodiac's jagged wheel
  Revolving still more near unto the Bears,
  Unless it swerved aside from its old track.

How that may be wouldst thou have power to think,
  Collected in thyself, imagine Zion
  Together with this mount on earth to stand,

So that they both one sole horizon have,
  And hemispheres diverse; whereby the road
  Which Phaeton, alas! knew not to drive,

Thou'lt see how of necessity must pass
  This on one side, when that upon the other,
  If thine intelligence right clearly heed."

"Truly, my Master," said I, "never yet
  Saw I so clearly as I now discern,
  There where my wit appeared incompetent,

That the mid-circle of supernal motion,
  Which in some art is the Equator called,
  And aye remains between the Sun and Winter,

For reason which thou sayest, departeth hence
  Tow'rds the Septentrion, what time the Hebrews
  Beheld it tow'rds the region of the heat.

But, if it pleaseth thee, I fain would learn
  How far we have to go; for the hill rises
  Higher than eyes of mine have power to rise."

And he to me: "This mount is such, that ever
  At the beginning down below 'tis tiresome,
  And aye the more one climbs, the less it hurts.

Therefore, when it shall seem so pleasant to thee,
  That going up shall be to thee as easy
  As going down the current in a boat,

Then at this pathway's ending thou wilt be;
  There to repose thy panting breath expect;
  No more I answer; and this I know for true."

And as he finished uttering these words,
  A voice close by us sounded: "Peradventure
  Thou wilt have need of sitting down ere that."

At sound thereof each one of us turned round,
  And saw upon the left hand a great rock,
  Which neither I nor he before had noticed.

Thither we drew; and there were persons there
  Who in the shadow stood behind the rock,
  As one through indolence is wont to stand.

And one of them, who seemed to me fatigued,
 Was sitting down, and both his knees embraced,
 Holding his face low down between them bowed.

"O my sweet Lord," I said, "do turn thine eye
 On him who shows himself more negligent
 Then even Sloth herself his sister were."

Then he turned round to us, and he gave heed,
 Just lifting up his eyes above his thigh,
 And said: "Now go thou up, for thou art valiant."

Then knew I who he was; and the distress,
 That still a little did my breathing quicken,
 My going to him hindered not; and after

I came to him he hardly raised his head,
 Saying: "Hast thou seen clearly how the sun
 O'er thy left shoulder drives his chariot?"

His sluggish attitude and his curt words
 A little unto laughter moved my lips;
 Then I began: "Belacqua, I grieve not

For thee henceforth; but tell me, wherefore seated
 In this place art thou? Waitest thou an escort?
 Or has thy usual habit seized upon thee?"

And he: "O brother, what's the use of climbing?
 Since to my torment would not let me go
 The Angel of God, who sitteth at the gate.

First heaven must needs so long revolve me round
 Outside thereof, as in my life it did,
 Since the good sighs I to the end postponed,

Unless, e'er that, some prayer may bring me aid
 Which rises from a heart that lives in grace;
 What profit others that in heaven are heard not?"

Meanwhile the Poet was before me mounting,
 And saying: "Come now; see the sun has touched
 Meridian, and from the shore the night

Covers already with her foot Morocco."

Canto V

I had already from those shades departed,
  And followed in the footsteps of my Guide,
  When from behind, pointing his finger at me,

One shouted: "See, it seems as if shone not
  The sunshine on the left of him below,
  And like one living seems he to conduct him."

Mine eyes I turned at utterance of these words,
  And saw them watching with astonishment
  But me, but me, and the light which was broken!

"Why doth thy mind so occupy itself,"
  The Master said, "that thou thy pace dost slacken?
  What matters it to thee what here is whispered?

Come after me, and let the people talk;
  Stand like a steadfast tower, that never wags
  Its top for all the blowing of the winds;

For evermore the man in whom is springing
  Thought upon thought, removes from him the mark,
  Because the force of one the other weakens."

What could I say in answer but "I come"?
  I said it somewhat with that color tinged
  Which makes a man of pardon sometimes worthy.

Meanwhile along the mountain-side across
  Came people in advance of us a little,
  Singing the Miserere verse by verse.

When they became aware I gave no place
  For passage of the sunshine through my body,
  They changed their song into a long, hoarse "Oh!"

And two of them, in form of messengers,
  Ran forth to meet us, and demanded of us,
  "Of your condition make us cognisant."

And said my Master: "Ye can go your way
  And carry back again to those who sent you,
  That this one's body is of very flesh.

If they stood still because they saw his shadow,
  As I suppose, enough is answered them;
  Him let them honor, it may profit them."

Vapours enkindled saw I ne'er so swiftly
  At early nightfall cleave the air serene,
  Nor, at the set of sun, the clouds of August,

But upward they returned in briefer time,
  And, on arriving, with the others wheeled
  Tow'rds us, like troops that run without a rein.

"This folk that presses unto us is great,
  And cometh to implore thee," said the Poet;
  "So still go onward, and in going listen."

"O soul that goest to beatitude
  With the same members wherewith thou wast born,"
  Shouting they came, "a little stay thy steps,

Look, if thou e'er hast any of us seen,
  So that o'er yonder thou bear news of him;
  Ah, why dost thou go on? Ah, why not stay?

Long since we all were slain by violence,
  And sinners even to the latest hour;
  Then did a light from heaven admonish us,

So that, both penitent and pardoning, forth
  From life we issued reconciled to God,
  Who with desire to see Him stirs our hearts."

And I: "Although I gaze into your faces,
  No one I recognize; but if may please you
  Aught I have power to do, ye well-born spirits,

Speak ye, and I will do it, by that peace
  Which, following the feet of such a Guide,
  From world to world makes itself sought by me."

And one began: "Each one has confidence
 In thy good offices without an oath,
 Unless the I cannot cut off the I will;

Whence I, who speak alone before the others,
 Pray thee, if ever thou dost see the land
 That 'twixt Romagna lies and that of Charles,

Thou be so courteous to me of thy prayers
 In Fano, that they pray for me devoutly,
 That I may purge away my grave offences.

From thence was I; but the deep wounds, through which
 Issued the blood wherein I had my seat,
 Were dealt me in bosom of the Antenori,

There where I thought to be the most secure;
 'Twas he of Este had it done, who held me
 In hatred far beyond what justice willed.

But if towards the Mira I had fled,
 When I was overtaken at Oriaco,
 I still should be o'er yonder where men breathe.

I ran to the lagoon, and reeds and mire
 Did so entangle me I fell, and saw there
 A lake made from my veins upon the ground."

Then said another: "Ah, be that desire
 Fulfilled that draws thee to the lofty mountain,
 As thou with pious pity aidest mine.

I was of Montefeltro, and am Buonconte;
 Giovanna, nor none other cares for me;
 Hence among these I go with downcast front."

And I to him: "What violence or what chance
 Led thee astray so far from Campaldino,
 That never has thy sepulture been known?"

"Oh," he replied, "at Casentino's foot
 A river crosses named Archiano, born
 Above the Hermitage in Apennine.

There where the name thereof becometh void
  Did I arrive, pierced through and through the throat,
  Fleeing on foot, and bloodying the plain;

There my sight lost I, and my utterance
  Ceased in the name of Mary, and thereat
  I fell, and tenantless my flesh remained.

Truth will I speak, repeat it to the living;
  God's Angel took me up, and he of hell
  Shouted: 'O thou from heaven, why dost thou rob me?

Thou bearest away the eternal part of him,
  For one poor little tear, that takes him from me;
  But with the rest I'll deal in other fashion!'

Well knowest thou how in the air is gathered
  That humid vapour which to water turns,
  Soon as it rises where the cold doth grasp it.

He joined that evil will, which aye seeks evil,
  To intellect, and moved the mist and wind
  By means of power, which his own nature gave;

Thereafter, when the day was spent, the valley
  From Pratomagno to the great yoke covered
  With fog, and made the heaven above intent,

So that the pregnant air to water changed;
  Down fell the rain, and to the gullies came
  Whate'er of it earth tolerated not;

And as it mingled with the mighty torrents,
  Towards the royal river with such speed
  It headlong rushed, that nothing held it back.

My frozen body near unto its outlet
  The robust Archian found, and into Arno
  Thrust it, and loosened from my breast the cross

I made of me, when agony o'ercame me;
  It rolled me on the banks and on the bottom,
  Then with its booty covered and begirt me."

"Ah, when thou hast returned unto the world,
And rested thee from thy long journeying,"
After the second followed the third spirit,

"Do thou remember me who am the Pia;
Siena made me, unmade me Maremma;
He knoweth it, who had encircled first,

Espousing me, my finger with his gem."

Canto VI

Whene'er is broken up the game of Zara,
He who has lost remains behind despondent,
The throws repeating, and in sadness learns;

The people with the other all depart;
One goes in front, and one behind doth pluck him,
And at his side one brings himself to mind;

He pauses not, and this and that one hears;
They crowd no more to whom his hand he stretches,
And from the throng he thus defends himself.

Even such was I in that dense multitude,
Turning to them this way and that my face,
And, promising, I freed myself therefrom.

There was the Aretine, who from the arms
Untamed of Ghin di Tacco had his death,
And he who fleeing from pursuit was drowned.

There was imploring with his hands outstretched
Frederick Novello, and that one of Pisa
Who made the good Marzucco seem so strong.

I saw Count Orso; and the soul divided
By hatred and by envy from its body,
As it declared, and not for crime committed,

Pierre de la Brosse I say; and here provide
While still on earth the Lady of Brabant,
So that for this she be of no worse flock!

As soon as I was free from all those shades
  Who only prayed that some one else may pray,
  So as to hasten their becoming holy,

Began I: "It appears that thou deniest,
  O light of mine, expressly in some text,
  That orison can bend decree of Heaven;

And ne'ertheless these people pray for this.
  Might then their expectation bootless be?
  Or is to me thy saying not quite clear?"

And he to me: "My writing is explicit,
  And not fallacious is the hope of these,
  If with sane intellect 'tis well regarded;

For top of judgment doth not vail itself,
  Because the fire of love fulfils at once
  What he must satisfy who here installs him.

And there, where I affirmed that proposition,
  Defect was not amended by a prayer,
  Because the prayer from God was separate.

Verily, in so deep a questioning
  Do not decide, unless she tell it thee,
  Who light 'twixt truth and intellect shall be.

I know not if thou understand; I speak
  Of Beatrice; her shalt thou see above,
  Smiling and happy, on this mountain's top."

And I: "Good Leader, let us make more haste,
  For I no longer tire me as before;
  And see, e'en now the hill a shadow casts."

"We will go forward with this day" he answered,
  "As far as now is possible for us;
  But otherwise the fact is than thou thinkest.

Ere thou art up there, thou shalt see return
  Him, who now hides himself behind the hill,
  So that thou dost not interrupt his rays.

But yonder there behold! a soul that stationed
  All, all alone is looking hitherward;
  It will point out to us the quickest way."

We came up unto it; O Lombard soul,
  How lofty and disdainful thou didst bear thee,
  And grand and slow in moving of thine eyes!

Nothing whatever did it say to us,
  But let us go our way, eying us only
  After the manner of a couchant lion;

Still near to it Virgilius drew, entreating
  That it would point us out the best ascent;
  And it replied not unto his demand,

But of our native land and of our life
  It questioned us; and the sweet Guide began:
  "Mantua,"—and the shade, all in itself recluse,

Rose tow'rds him from the place where first it was,
  Saying: "O Mantuan, I am Sordello
  Of thine own land!" and one embraced the other.

Ah! servile Italy, grief's hostelry!
  A ship without a pilot in great tempest!
  No Lady thou of Provinces, but brothel!

That noble soul was so impatient, only
  At the sweet sound of his own native land,
  To make its citizen glad welcome there;

And now within thee are not without war
  Thy living ones, and one doth gnaw the other
  Of those whom one wall and one fosse shut in!

Search, wretched one, all round about the shores
  Thy seaboard, and then look within thy bosom,
  If any part of thee enjoyeth peace!

What boots it, that for thee Justinian
  The bridle mend, if empty be the saddle?
  Withouten this the shame would be the less.

Ah! people, thou that oughtest to be devout,
  And to let Caesar sit upon the saddle,
  If well thou hearest what God teacheth thee,

Behold how fell this wild beast has become,
  Being no longer by the spur corrected,
  Since thou hast laid thy hand upon the bridle.

O German Albert! who abandonest
  Her that has grown recalcitrant and savage,
  And oughtest to bestride her saddle-bow,

May a just judgment from the stars down fall
  Upon thy blood, and be it new and open,
  That thy successor may have fear thereof;

Because thy father and thyself have suffered,
  By greed of those transalpine lands distrained,
  The garden of the empire to be waste.

Come and behold Montecchi and Cappelletti,
  Monaldi and Fillippeschi, careless man!
  Those sad already, and these doubt-depressed!

Come, cruel one! come and behold the oppression
  Of thy nobility, and cure their wounds,
  And thou shalt see how safe is Santafiore!

Come and behold thy Rome, that is lamenting,
  Widowed, alone, and day and night exclaims,
  "My Caesar, why hast thou forsaken me?"

Come and behold how loving are the people;
  And if for us no pity moveth thee,
  Come and be made ashamed of thy renown!

And if it lawful be, O Jove Supreme!
  Who upon earth for us wast crucified,
  Are thy just eyes averted otherwhere?

Or preparation is 't, that, in the abyss
  Of thine own counsel, for some good thou makest
  From our perception utterly cut off?

For all the towns of Italy are full
  Of tyrants, and becometh a Marcellus
  Each peasant churl who plays the partisan!

My Florence! well mayst thou contented be
  With this digression, which concerns thee not,
  Thanks to thy people who such forethought take!

Many at heart have justice, but shoot slowly,
  That unadvised they come not to the bow,
  But on their very lips thy people have it!

Many refuse to bear the common burden;
  But thy solicitous people answereth
  Without being asked, and crieth: "I submit."

Now be thou joyful, for thou hast good reason;
  Thou affluent, thou in peace, thou full of wisdom!
  If I speak true, the event conceals it not.

Athens and Lacedaemon, they who made
  The ancient laws, and were so civilized,
  Made towards living well a little sign

Compared with thee, who makest such fine-spun
  Provisions, that to middle of November
  Reaches not what thou in October spinnest.

How oft, within the time of thy remembrance,
  Laws, money, offices, and usages
  Hast thou remodelled, and renewed thy members?

And if thou mind thee well, and see the light,
  Thou shalt behold thyself like a sick woman,
  Who cannot find repose upon her down,

But by her tossing wardeth off her pain.

Canto VII

After the gracious and glad salutations
  Had three and four times been reiterated,
  Sordello backward drew and said, "Who are you?"

"Or ever to this mountain were directed
  The souls deserving to ascend to God,
  My bones were buried by Octavian.

I am Virgilius; and for no crime else
  Did I lose heaven, than for not having faith;"
  In this wise then my Leader made reply.

As one who suddenly before him sees
  Something whereat he marvels, who believes
  And yet does not, saying, "It is! it is not!"

So he appeared; and then bowed down his brow,
  And with humility returned towards him,
  And, where inferiors embrace, embraced him.

"O glory of the Latians, thou," he said,
  "Through whom our language showed what it could do
  O pride eternal of the place I came from,

What merit or what grace to me reveals thee?
  If I to hear thy words be worthy, tell me
  If thou dost come from Hell, and from what cloister."

"Through all the circles of the doleful realm,"
  Responded he, "have I come hitherward;
  Heaven's power impelled me, and with that I come.

I by not doing, not by doing, lost
  The sight of that high sun which thou desirest,
  And which too late by me was recognized.

A place there is below not sad with torments,
  But darkness only, where the lamentations
  Have not the sound of wailing, but are sighs.

There dwell I with the little innocents
  Snatched by the teeth of Death, or ever they
  Were from our human sinfulness exempt.

There dwell I among those who the three saintly
  Virtues did not put on, and without vice
  The others knew and followed all of them.

But if thou know and can, some indication
　Give us by which we may the sooner come
　Where Purgatory has its right beginning."

He answered: "No fixed place has been assigned us;
　'Tis lawful for me to go up and round;
　So far as I can go, as guide I join thee.

But see already how the day declines,
　And to go up by night we are not able;
　Therefore 'tis well to think of some fair sojourn.

Souls are there on the right hand here withdrawn;
　If thou permit me I will lead thee to them,
　And thou shalt know them not without delight."

"How is this?" was the answer; "should one wish
　To mount by night would he prevented be
　By others? or mayhap would not have power?"

And on the ground the good Sordello drew
　His finger, saying, "See, this line alone
　Thou couldst not pass after the sun is gone;

Not that aught else would hindrance give, however,
　To going up, save the nocturnal darkness;
　This with the want of power the will perplexes.

We might indeed therewith return below,
　And, wandering, walk the hill-side round about,
　While the horizon holds the day imprisoned."

Thereon my Lord, as if in wonder, said:
　"Do thou conduct us thither, where thou sayest
　That we can take delight in tarrying."

Little had we withdrawn us from that place,
　When I perceived the mount was hollowed out
　In fashion as the valleys here are hollowed.

"Thitherward," said that shade, "will we repair,
　Where of itself the hill-side makes a lap,
　And there for the new day will we await."

'Twixt hill and plain there was a winding path
  Which led us to the margin of that dell,
  Where dies the border more than half away.

Gold and fine silver, and scarlet and pearl-white,
  The Indian wood resplendent and serene,
  Fresh emerald the moment it is broken,

By herbage and by flowers within that hollow
  Planted, each one in color would be vanquished,
  As by its greater vanquished is the less.

Nor in that place had nature painted only,
  But of the sweetness of a thousand odours
  Made there a mingled fragrance and unknown.

"Salve Regina," on the green and flowers
  There seated, singing, spirits I beheld,
  Which were not visible outside the valley.

"Before the scanty sun now seeks his nest,"
  Began the Mantuan who had led us thither,
  "Among them do not wish me to conduct you.

Better from off this ledge the acts and faces
  Of all of them will you discriminate,
  Than in the plain below received among them.

He who sits highest, and the semblance bears
  Of having what he should have done neglected,
  And to the others' song moves not his lips,

Rudolph the Emperor was, who had the power
  To heal the wounds that Italy have slain,
  So that through others slowly she revives.

The other, who in look doth comfort him,
  Governed the region where the water springs,
  The Moldau bears the Elbe, and Elbe the sea.

His name was Ottocar; and in swaddling-clothes
  Far better he than bearded Winceslaus
  His son, who feeds in luxury and ease.

And the small-nosed, who close in council seems
  With him that has an aspect so benign,
  Died fleeing and disflowering the lily;

Look there, how he is beating at his breast!
  Behold the other one, who for his cheek
  Sighing has made of his own palm a bed;

Father and father-in-law of France's Pest
  Are they, and know his vicious life and lewd,
  And hence proceeds the grief that so doth pierce them.

He who appears so stalwart, and chimes in,
  Singing, with that one of the manly nose,
  The cord of every valour wore begirt;

And if as King had after him remained
  The stripling who in rear of him is sitting,
  Well had the valour passed from vase to vase,

Which cannot of the other heirs be said.
  Frederick and Jacomo possess the realms,
  But none the better heritage possesses.

Not oftentimes upriseth through the branches
  The probity of man; and this He wills
  Who gives it, so that we may ask of Him.

Eke to the large-nosed reach my words, no less
  Than to the other, Pier, who with him sings;
  Whence Provence and Apulia grieve already

The plant is as inferior to its seed,
  As more than Beatrice and Margaret
  Costanza boasteth of her husband still.

Behold the monarch of the simple life,
  Harry of England, sitting there alone;
  He in his branches has a better issue.

He who the lowest on the ground among them
  Sits looking upward, is the Marquis William,
  For whose sake Alessandria and her war

Make Monferrat and Canavese weep."

Canto VIII

'Twas now the hour that turneth back desire
  In those who sail the sea, and melts the heart,
  The day they've said to their sweet friends farewell,

And the new pilgrim penetrates with love,
  If he doth hear from far away a bell
  That seemeth to deplore the dying day,

When I began to make of no avail
  My hearing, and to watch one of the souls
  Uprisen, that begged attention with its hand.

It joined and lifted upward both its palms,
  Fixing its eyes upon the orient,
  As if it said to God, "Naught else I care for."

"Te lucis ante" so devoutly issued
  Forth from its mouth, and with such dulcet notes,
  It made me issue forth from my own mind.

And then the others, sweetly and devoutly,
  Accompanied it through all the hymn entire,
  Having their eyes on the supernal wheels.

Here, Reader, fix thine eyes well on the truth,
  For now indeed so subtile is the veil,
  Surely to penetrate within is easy.

I saw that army of the gentle-born
  Thereafterward in silence upward gaze,
  As if in expectation, pale and humble;

And from on high come forth and down descend,
  I saw two Angels with two flaming swords,
  Truncated and deprived of their points.

Green as the little leaflets just now born
  Their garments were, which, by their verdant pinions
  Beaten and blown abroad, they trailed behind.

One just above us came to take his station,
  And one descended to the opposite bank,
  So that the people were contained between them.

Clearly in them discerned I the blond head;
  But in their faces was the eye bewildered,
  As faculty confounded by excess.

"From Mary's bosom both of them have come,"
  Sordello said, "as guardians of the valley
  Against the serpent, that will come anon."

Whereupon I, who knew not by what road,
  Turned round about, and closely drew myself,
  Utterly frozen, to the faithful shoulders.

And once again Sordello: "Now descend we
  'Mid the grand shades, and we will speak to them;
  Right pleasant will it be for them to see you."

Only three steps I think that I descended,
  And was below, and saw one who was looking
  Only at me, as if he fain would know me.

Already now the air was growing dark,
  But not so that between his eyes and mine
  It did not show what it before locked up.

Tow'rds me he moved, and I tow'rds him did move;
  Noble Judge Nino! how it me delighted,
  When I beheld thee not among the damned!

No greeting fair was left unsaid between us;
  Then asked he: "How long is it since thou camest
  O'er the far waters to the mountain's foot?"

"Oh!" said I to him, "through the dismal places
  I came this morn; and am in the first life,
  Albeit the other, going thus, I gain."

And on the instant my reply was heard,
  He and Sordello both shrank back from me,
  Like people who are suddenly bewildered.

One to Virgilius, and the other turned
  To one who sat there, crying, "Up, Currado!
  Come and behold what God in grace has willed!"

Then, turned to me: "By that especial grace
  Thou owest unto Him, who so conceals
  His own first wherefore, that it has no ford,

When thou shalt be beyond the waters wide,
  Tell my Giovanna that she pray for me,
  Where answer to the innocent is made.

I do not think her mother loves me more,
  Since she has laid aside her wimple white,
  Which she, unhappy, needs must wish again.

Through her full easily is comprehended
  How long in woman lasts the fire of love,
  If eye or touch do not relight it often.

So fair a hatchment will not make for her
  The Viper marshalling the Milanese
  A-field, as would have made Gallura's Cock."

In this wise spake he, with the stamp impressed
  Upon his aspect of that righteous zeal
  Which measurably burneth in the heart.

My greedy eyes still wandered up to heaven,
  Still to that point where slowest are the stars,
  Even as a wheel the nearest to its axle.

And my Conductor: "Son, what dost thou gaze at
  Up there?" And I to him: "At those three torches
  With which this hither pole is all on fire."

And he to me: "The four resplendent stars
  Thou sawest this morning are down yonder low,
  And these have mounted up to where those were."

As he was speaking, to himself Sordello
  Drew him, and said, "Lo there our Adversary!"
  And pointed with his finger to look thither.

Upon the side on which the little valley
  No barrier hath, a serpent was; perchance
  The same which gave to Eve the bitter food.

'Twixt grass and flowers came on the evil streak,
  Turning at times its head about, and licking
  Its back like to a beast that smoothes itself.

I did not see, and therefore cannot say
  How the celestial falcons 'gan to move,
  But well I saw that they were both in motion.

Hearing the air cleft by their verdant wings,
  The serpent fled, and round the Angels wheeled,
  Up to their stations flying back alike.

The shade that to the Judge had near approached
  When he had called, throughout that whole assault
  Had not a moment loosed its gaze on me.

"So may the light that leadeth thee on high
  Find in thine own free-will as much of wax
  As needful is up to the highest azure,"

Began it, "if some true intelligence
  Of Valdimagra or its neighborhood
  Thou knowest, tell it me, who once was great there.

Currado Malaspina was I called;
  I'm not the elder, but from him descended;
  To mine I bore the love which here refineth."

"O," said I unto him, "through your domains
  I never passed, but where is there a dwelling
  Throughout all Europe, where they are not known?

That fame, which doeth honor to your house,
  Proclaims its Signors and proclaims its land,
  So that he knows of them who ne'er was there.

And, as I hope for heaven, I swear to you
  Your honored family in naught abates
  The glory of the purse and of the sword.

It is so privileged by use and nature,
  That though a guilty head misguide the world,
  Sole it goes right, and scorns the evil way."

And he: "Now go; for the sun shall not lie
  Seven times upon the pillow which the Ram
  With all his four feet covers and bestrides,

Before that such a courteous opinion
  Shall in the middle of thy head be nailed
  With greater nails than of another's speech,

Unless the course of justice standeth still."

Canto IX

The concubine of old Tithonus now
  Gleamed white upon the eastern balcony,
  Forth from the arms of her sweet paramour;

With gems her forehead all relucent was,
  Set in the shape of that cold animal
  Which with its tail doth smite amain the nations,

And of the steps, with which she mounts, the Night
  Had taken two in that place where we were,
  And now the third was bending down its wings;

When I, who something had of Adam in me,
  Vanquished by sleep, upon the grass reclined,
  There were all five of us already sat.

Just at the hour when her sad lay begins
  The little swallow, near unto the morning,
  Perchance in memory of her former woes,

And when the mind of man, a wanderer
  More from the flesh, and less by thought imprisoned,
  Almost prophetic in its visions is,

In dreams it seemed to me I saw suspended
  An eagle in the sky, with plumes of gold,
  With wings wide open, and intent to stoop,

And this, it seemed to me, was where had been
　By Ganymede his kith and kin abandoned,
　When to the high consistory he was rapt.

I thought within myself, perchance he strikes
　From habit only here, and from elsewhere
　Disdains to bear up any in his feet.

Then wheeling somewhat more, it seemed to me,
　Terrible as the lightning he descended,
　And snatched me upward even to the fire.

Therein it seemed that he and I were burning,
　And the imagined fire did scorch me so,
　That of necessity my sleep was broken.

Not otherwise Achilles started up,
　Around him turning his awakened eyes,
　And knowing not the place in which he was,

What time from Chiron stealthily his mother
　Carried him sleeping in her arms to Scyros,
　Wherefrom the Greeks withdrew him afterwards,

Than I upstarted, when from off my face
　Sleep fled away; and pallid I became,
　As doth the man who freezes with affright.

Only my Comforter was at my side,
　And now the sun was more than two hours high,
　And turned towards the sea-shore was my face.

"Be not intimidated," said my Lord,
　"Be reassured, for all is well with us;
　Do not restrain, but put forth all thy strength.

Thou hast at length arrived at Purgatory;
　See there the cliff that closes it around;
　See there the entrance, where it seems disjoined.

Whilom at dawn, which doth precede the day,
　When inwardly thy spirit was asleep
　Upon the flowers that deck the land below,

There came a Lady and said: 'I am Lucia;
  Let me take this one up, who is asleep;
  So will I make his journey easier for him.'

Sordello and the other noble shapes
  Remained; she took thee, and, as day grew bright,
  Upward she came, and I upon her footsteps.

She laid thee here; and first her beauteous eyes
  That open entrance pointed out to me;
  Then she and sleep together went away."

In guise of one whose doubts are reassured,
  And who to confidence his fear doth change,
  After the truth has been discovered to him,

So did I change; and when without disquiet
  My Leader saw me, up along the cliff
  He moved, and I behind him, tow'rd the height.

Reader, thou seest well how I exalt
  My theme, and therefore if with greater art
  I fortify it, marvel not thereat.

Nearer approached we, and were in such place,
  That there, where first appeared to me a rift
  Like to a crevice that disparts a wall,

I saw a portal, and three stairs beneath,
  Diverse in color, to go up to it,
  And a gate-keeper, who yet spake no word.

And as I opened more and more mine eyes,
  I saw him seated on the highest stair,
  Such in the face that I endured it not.

And in his hand he had a naked sword,
  Which so reflected back the sunbeams tow'rds us,
  That oft in vain I lifted up mine eyes.

"Tell it from where you are, what is't you wish?"
  Began he to exclaim; "where is the escort?
  Take heed your coming hither harm you not!"

"A Lady of Heaven, with these things conversant,"
 My Master answered him, "but even now
 Said to us, 'Thither go; there is the portal.'"

"And may she speed your footsteps in all good,"
 Again began the courteous janitor;
 "Come forward then unto these stairs of ours."

Thither did we approach; and the first stair
 Was marble white, so polished and so smooth,
 I mirrored myself therein as I appear.

The second, tinct of deeper hue than perse,
 Was of a calcined and uneven stone,
 Cracked all asunder lengthwise and across.

The third, that uppermost rests massively,
 Porphyry seemed to me, as flaming red
 As blood that from a vein is spirting forth.

Both of his feet was holding upon this
 The Angel of God, upon the threshold seated,
 Which seemed to me a stone of diamond.

Along the three stairs upward with good will
 Did my Conductor draw me, saying: "Ask
 Humbly that he the fastening may undo."

Devoutly at the holy feet I cast me,
 For mercy's sake besought that he would open,
 But first upon my breast three times I smote.

Seven P's upon my forehead he described
 With the sword's point, and, "Take heed that thou wash
 These wounds, when thou shalt be within," he said.

Ashes, or earth that dry is excavated,
 Of the same color were with his attire,
 And from beneath it he drew forth two keys.

One was of gold, and the other was of silver;
 First with the white, and after with the yellow,
 Plied he the door, so that I was content.

"Whenever faileth either of these keys
  So that it turn not rightly in the lock,"
  He said to us, "this entrance doth not open.

More precious one is, but the other needs
  More art and intellect ere it unlock,
  For it is that which doth the knot unloose.

From Peter I have them; and he bade me err
  Rather in opening than in keeping shut,
  If people but fall down before my feet."

Then pushed the portals of the sacred door,
  Exclaiming: "Enter; but I give you warning
  That forth returns whoever looks behind."

And when upon their hinges were turned round
  The swivels of that consecrated gate,
  Which are of metal, massive and sonorous,

Roared not so loud, nor so discordant seemed
  Tarpeia, when was ta'en from it the good
  Metellus, wherefore meagre it remained.

At the first thunder-peal I turned attentive,
  And "Te Deum laudamus" seemed to hear
  In voices mingled with sweet melody.

Exactly such an image rendered me
  That which I heard, as we are wont to catch,
  When people singing with the organ stand;

For now we hear, and now hear not, the words.

Canto X

When we had crossed the threshold of the door
  Which the perverted love of souls disuses,
  Because it makes the crooked way seem straight,

Re-echoing I heard it closed again;
  And if I had turned back mine eyes upon it,
  What for my failing had been fit excuse?

We mounted upward through a rifted rock,
  Which undulated to this side and that,
  Even as a wave receding and advancing.

"Here it behoves us use a little art,"
  Began my Leader, "to adapt ourselves
  Now here, now there, to the receding side."

And this our footsteps so infrequent made,
  That sooner had the moon's decreasing disk
  Regained its bed to sink again to rest,

Than we were forth from out that needle's eye;
  But when we free and in the open were,
  There where the mountain backward piles itself,

I wearied out, and both of us uncertain
  About our way, we stopped upon a plain
  More desolate than roads across the deserts.

From where its margin borders on the void,
  To foot of the high bank that ever rises,
  A human body three times told would measure;

And far as eye of mine could wing its flight,
  Now on the left, and on the right flank now,
  The same this cornice did appear to me.

Thereon our feet had not been moved as yet,
  When I perceived the embankment round about,
  Which all right of ascent had interdicted,

To be of marble white, and so adorned
  With sculptures, that not only Polycletus,
  But Nature's self, had there been put to shame.

The Angel, who came down to earth with tidings
  Of peace, that had been wept for many a year,
  And opened Heaven from its long interdict,

In front of us appeared so truthfully
  There sculptured in a gracious attitude,
  He did not seem an image that is silent.

One would have sworn that he was saying, "Ave;"
  For she was there in effigy portrayed
  Who turned the key to ope the exalted love,

And in her mien this language had impressed,
  "Ecce ancilla Dei," as distinctly
  As any figure stamps itself in wax.

"Keep not thy mind upon one place alone,"
  The gentle Master said, who had me standing
  Upon that side where people have their hearts;

Whereat I moved mine eyes, and I beheld
  In rear of Mary, and upon that side
  Where he was standing who conducted me,

Another story on the rock imposed;
  Wherefore I passed Virgilius and drew near,
  So that before mine eyes it might be set.

There sculptured in the self-same marble were
  The cart and oxen, drawing the holy ark,
  Wherefore one dreads an office not appointed.

People appeared in front, and all of them
  In seven choirs divided, of two senses
  Made one say "No," the other, "Yes, they sing."

Likewise unto the smoke of the frankincense,
  Which there was imaged forth, the eyes and nose
  Were in the yes and no discordant made.

Preceded there the vessel benedight,
  Dancing with girded loins, the humble Psalmist,
  And more and less than King was he in this.

Opposite, represented at the window
  Of a great palace, Michal looked upon him,
  Even as a woman scornful and afflicted.

I moved my feet from where I had been standing,
  To examine near at hand another story,
  Which after Michal glimmered white upon me.

There the high glory of the Roman Prince
  Was chronicled, whose great beneficence
  Moved Gregory to his great victory;

'Tis of the Emperor Trajan I am speaking;
  And a poor widow at his bridle stood,
  In attitude of weeping and of grief.

Around about him seemed it thronged and full
  Of cavaliers, and the eagles in the gold
  Above them visibly in the wind were moving.

The wretched woman in the midst of these
  Seemed to be saying: "Give me vengeance, Lord,
  For my dead son, for whom my heart is breaking."

And he to answer her: "Now wait until
  I shall return." And she: "My Lord," like one
  In whom grief is impatient, "shouldst thou not

Return?" And he: "Who shall be where I am
  Will give it thee." And she: "Good deed of others
  What boots it thee, if thou neglect thine own?"

Whence he: "Now comfort thee, for it behoves me
  That I discharge my duty ere I move;
  Justice so wills, and pity doth retain me."

He who on no new thing has ever looked
  Was the creator of this visible language,
  Novel to us, for here it is not found.

While I delighted me in contemplating
  The images of such humility,
  And dear to look on for their Maker's sake,

"Behold, upon this side, but rare they make
  Their steps," the Poet murmured, "many people;
  These will direct us to the lofty stairs."

Mine eyes, that in beholding were intent
  To see new things, of which they curious are,
  In turning round towards him were not slow.

But still I wish not, Reader, thou shouldst swerve
　From thy good purposes, because thou hearest
　How God ordaineth that the debt be paid;

Attend not to the fashion of the torment,
　Think of what follows; think that at the worst
　It cannot reach beyond the mighty sentence.

"Master," began I, "that which I behold
　Moving towards us seems to me not persons,
　And what I know not, so in sight I waver."

And he to me: "The grievous quality
　Of this their torment bows them so to earth,
　That my own eyes at first contended with it;

But look there fixedly, and disentangle
　By sight what cometh underneath those stones;
　Already canst thou see how each is stricken."

O ye proud Christians! wretched, weary ones!
　Who, in the vision of the mind infirm
　Confidence have in your backsliding steps,

Do ye not comprehend that we are worms,
　Born to bring forth the angelic butterfly
　That flieth unto judgment without screen?

Why floats aloft your spirit high in air?
　Like are ye unto insects undeveloped,
　Even as the worm in whom formation fails!

As to sustain a ceiling or a roof,
　In place of corbel, oftentimes a figure
　Is seen to join its knees unto its breast,

Which makes of the unreal real anguish
　Arise in him who sees it, fashioned thus
　Beheld I those, when I had ta'en good heed.

True is it, they were more or less bent down,
　According as they more or less were laden;
　And he who had most patience in his looks

Weeping did seem to say, "I can no more!"

Canto XI

"Our Father, thou who dwellest in the heavens,
  Not circumscribed, but from the greater love
  Thou bearest to the first effects on high,

Praised be thy name and thine omnipotence
  By every creature, as befitting is
  To render thanks to thy sweet effluence.

Come unto us the peace of thy dominion,
  For unto it we cannot of ourselves,
  If it come not, with all our intellect.

Even as thine own Angels of their will
  Make sacrifice to thee, Hosanna singing,
  So may all men make sacrifice of theirs.

Give unto us this day our daily manna,
  Withouten which in this rough wilderness
  Backward goes he who toils most to advance.

And even as we the trespass we have suffered
  Pardon in one another, pardon thou
  Benignly, and regard not our desert.

Our virtue, which is easily o'ercome,
  Put not to proof with the old Adversary,
  But thou from him who spurs it so, deliver.

This last petition verily, dear Lord,
  Not for ourselves is made, who need it not,
  But for their sake who have remained behind us."

Thus for themselves and us good furtherance
  Those shades imploring, went beneath a weight
  Like unto that of which we sometimes dream,

Unequally in anguish round and round
  And weary all, upon that foremost cornice,
  Purging away the smoke-stains of the world.

If there good words are always said for us,
  What may not here be said and done for them,
  By those who have a good root to their will?

Well may we help them wash away the marks
  That hence they carried, so that clean and light
  They may ascend unto the starry wheels!

"Ah! so may pity and justice you disburden
  Soon, that ye may have power to move the wing,
  That shall uplift you after your desire,

Show us on which hand tow'rd the stairs the way
  Is shortest, and if more than one the passes,
  Point us out that which least abruptly falls;

For he who cometh with me, through the burden
  Of Adam's flesh wherewith he is invested,
  Against his will is chary of his climbing."

The words of theirs which they returned to those
  That he whom I was following had spoken,
  It was not manifest from whom they came,

But it was said: "To the right hand come with us
  Along the bank, and ye shall find a pass
  Possible for living person to ascend.

And were I not impeded by the stone,
  Which this proud neck of mine doth subjugate,
  Whence I am forced to hold my visage down,

Him, who still lives and does not name himself,
  Would I regard, to see if I may know him
  And make him piteous unto this burden.

A Latian was I, and born of a great Tuscan;
  Guglielmo Aldobrandeschi was my father;
  I know not if his name were ever with you.

The ancient blood and deeds of gallantry
  Of my progenitors so arrogant made me
  That, thinking not upon the common mother,

All men I held in scorn to such extent
  I died therefor, as know the Sienese,
  And every child in Campagnatico.

I am Omberto; and not to me alone
  Has pride done harm, but all my kith and kin
  Has with it dragged into adversity.

And here must I this burden bear for it
  Till God be satisfied, since I did not
  Among the living, here among the dead."

Listening I downward bent my countenance;
  And one of them, not this one who was speaking,
  Twisted himself beneath the weight that cramps him,

And looked at me, and knew me, and called out,
  Keeping his eyes laboriously fixed
  On me, who all bowed down was going with them.

"O," asked I him, "art thou not Oderisi,
  Agobbio's honor, and honor of that art
  Which is in Paris called illuminating?"

"Brother," said he, "more laughing are the leaves
  Touched by the brush of Franco Bolognese;
  All his the honor now, and mine in part.

In sooth I had not been so courteous
  While I was living, for the great desire
  Of excellence, on which my heart was bent.

Here of such pride is paid the forfeiture;
  And yet I should not be here, were it not
  That, having power to sin, I turned to God.

O thou vain glory of the human powers,
  How little green upon thy summit lingers,
  If't be not followed by an age of grossness!

In painting Cimabue thought that he
  Should hold the field, now Giotto has the cry,
  So that the other's fame is growing dim.

So has one Guido from the other taken
  The glory of our tongue, and he perchance
  Is born, who from the nest shall chase them both.

Naught is this mundane rumour but a breath
  Of wind, that comes now this way and now that,
  And changes name, because it changes side.

What fame shalt thou have more, if old peel off
  From thee thy flesh, than if thou hadst been dead
  Before thou left the 'pappo' and the 'dindi,'

Ere pass a thousand years? which is a shorter
  Space to the eterne, than twinkling of an eye
  Unto the circle that in heaven wheels slowest.

With him, who takes so little of the road
  In front of me, all Tuscany resounded;
  And now he scarce is lisped of in Siena,

Where he was lord, what time was overthrown
  The Florentine delirium, that superb
  Was at that day as now 'tis prostitute.

Your reputation is the color of grass
  Which comes and goes, and that discolors it
  By which it issues green from out the earth."

And I: "Thy true speech fills my heart with good
  Humility, and great tumour thou assuagest;
  But who is he, of whom just now thou spakest?"

"That," he replied, "is Provenzan Salvani,
  And he is here because he had presumed
  To bring Siena all into his hands.

He has gone thus, and goeth without rest
  E'er since he died; such money renders back
  In payment he who is on earth too daring."

And I: "If every spirit who awaits
  The verge of life before that he repent,
  Remains below there and ascends not hither,

(Unless good orison shall him bestead,)
  Until as much time as he lived be passed,
  How was the coming granted him in largess?"

"When he in greatest splendor lived," said he,
  "Freely upon the Campo of Siena,
  All shame being laid aside, he placed himself;

And there to draw his friend from the duress
  Which in the prison-house of Charles he suffered,
  He brought himself to tremble in each vein.

I say no more, and know that I speak darkly;
  Yet little time shall pass before thy neighbors
  Will so demean themselves that thou canst gloss it.

This action has released him from those confines."

Canto XII

Abreast, like oxen going in a yoke,
  I with that heavy-laden soul went on,
  As long as the sweet pedagogue permitted;

But when he said, "Leave him, and onward pass,
  For here 'tis good that with the sail and oars,
  As much as may be, each push on his barque;"

Upright, as walking wills it, I redressed
  My person, notwithstanding that my thoughts
  Remained within me downcast and abashed.

I had moved on, and followed willingly
  The footsteps of my Master, and we both
  Already showed how light of foot we were,

When unto me he said: "Cast down thine eyes;
  'Twere well for thee, to alleviate the way,
  To look upon the bed beneath thy feet."

As, that some memory may exist of them,
  Above the buried dead their tombs in earth
  Bear sculptured on them what they were before;

Whence often there we weep for them afresh,
  From pricking of remembrance, which alone
  To the compassionate doth set its spur;

So saw I there, but of a better semblance
  In point of artifice, with figures covered
  Whate'er as pathway from the mount projects.

I saw that one who was created noble
  More than all other creatures, down from heaven
  Flaming with lightnings fall upon one side.

I saw Briareus smitten by the dart
  Celestial, lying on the other side,
  Heavy upon the earth by mortal frost.

I saw Thymbraeus, Pallas saw, and Mars,
  Still clad in armor round about their father,
  Gaze at the scattered members of the giants.

I saw, at foot of his great labour, Nimrod,
  As if bewildered, looking at the people
  Who had been proud with him in Sennaar.

O Niobe! with what afflicted eyes
  Thee I beheld upon the pathway traced,
  Between thy seven and seven children slain!

O Saul! how fallen upon thy proper sword
  Didst thou appear there lifeless in Gilboa,
  That felt thereafter neither rain nor dew!

O mad Arachne! so I thee beheld
  E'en then half spider, sad upon the shreds
  Of fabric wrought in evil hour for thee!

O Rehoboam! no more seems to threaten
  Thine image there; but full of consternation
  A chariot bears it off, when none pursues!

Displayed moreo'er the adamantine pavement
  How unto his own mother made Alcmaeon
  Costly appear the luckless ornament;

Displayed how his own sons did throw themselves
  Upon Sennacherib within the temple,
  And how, he being dead, they left him there;

Displayed the ruin and the cruel carnage
  That Tomyris wrought, when she to Cyrus said,
  "Blood didst thou thirst for, and with blood I glut thee!"

Displayed how routed fled the Assyrians
  After that Holofernes had been slain,
  And likewise the remainder of that slaughter.

I saw there Troy in ashes and in caverns;
  O Ilion! thee, how abject and debased,
  Displayed the image that is there discerned!

Whoe'er of pencil master was or stile,
  That could portray the shades and traits which there
  Would cause each subtile genius to admire?

Dead seemed the dead, the living seemed alive;
  Better than I saw not who saw the truth,
  All that I trod upon while bowed I went.

Now wax ye proud, and on with looks uplifted,
  Ye sons of Eve, and bow not down your faces
  So that ye may behold your evil ways!

More of the mount by us was now encompassed,
  And far more spent the circuit of the sun,
  Than had the mind preoccupied imagined,

When he, who ever watchful in advance
  Was going on, began: "Lift up thy head,
  'Tis no more time to go thus meditating.

Lo there an Angel who is making haste
  To come towards us; lo, returning is
  From service of the day the sixth handmaiden.

With reverence thine acts and looks adorn,
  So that he may delight to speed us upward;
  Think that this day will never dawn again."

I was familiar with his admonition
  Ever to lose no time; so on this theme
  He could not unto me speak covertly.

Towards us came the being beautiful
  Vested in white, and in his countenance
  Such as appears the tremulous morning star.

His arms he opened, and opened then his wings;
  "Come," said he, "near at hand here are the steps,
  And easy from henceforth is the ascent."

At this announcement few are they who come!
  O human creatures, born to soar aloft,
  Why fall ye thus before a little wind?

He led us on to where the rock was cleft;
  There smote upon my forehead with his wings,
  Then a safe passage promised unto me.

As on the right hand, to ascend the mount
  Where seated is the church that lordeth it
  O'er the well-guided, above Rubaconte,

The bold abruptness of the ascent is broken
  By stairways that were made there in the age
  When still were safe the ledger and the stave,

E'en thus attempered is the bank which falls
  Sheer downward from the second circle there;
  But on this, side and that the high rock graze.

As we were turning thitherward our persons,
  "Beati pauperes spiritu," voices
  Sang in such wise that speech could tell it not.

Ah me! how different are these entrances
  From the Infernal! for with anthems here
  One enters, and below with wild laments.

We now were hunting up the sacred stairs,
  And it appeared to me by far more easy
  Than on the plain it had appeared before.

Whence I: "My Master, say, what heavy thing
 Has been uplifted from me, so that hardly
 Aught of fatigue is felt by me in walking?"

He answered: "When the P's which have remained
 Still on thy face almost obliterate
 Shall wholly, as the first is, be erased,

Thy feet will be so vanquished by good will,
 That not alone they shall not feel fatigue,
 But urging up will be to them delight."

Then did I even as they do who are going
 With something on the head to them unknown,
 Unless the signs of others make them doubt,

Wherefore the hand to ascertain is helpful,
 And seeks and finds, and doth fulfill the office
 Which cannot be accomplished by the sight;

And with the fingers of the right hand spread
 I found but six the letters, that had carved
 Upon my temples he who bore the keys;

Upon beholding which my Leader smiled.

Canto XIII

We were upon the summit of the stairs,
 Where for the second time is cut away
 The mountain, which ascending shriveth all.

There in like manner doth a cornice bind
 The hill all round about, as does the first,
 Save that its arc more suddenly is curved.

Shade is there none, nor sculpture that appears;
 So seems the bank, and so the road seems smooth,
 With but the livid color of the stone.

"If to inquire we wait for people here,"
 The Poet said, "I fear that peradventure
 Too much delay will our election have."

Then steadfast on the sun his eyes he fixed,
  Made his right side the centre of his motion,
  And turned the left part of himself about.

"O thou sweet light! with trust in whom I enter
  Upon this novel journey, do thou lead us,"
  Said he, "as one within here should be led.

Thou warmest the world, thou shinest over it;
  If other reason prompt not otherwise,
  Thy rays should evermore our leaders be!"

As much as here is counted for a mile,
  So much already there had we advanced
  In little time, by dint of ready will;

And tow'rds us there were heard to fly, albeit
  They were not visible, spirits uttering
  Unto Love's table courteous invitations,

The first voice that passed onward in its flight,
  "Vinum non habent," said in accents loud,
  And went reiterating it behind us.

And ere it wholly grew inaudible
  Because of distance, passed another, crying,
  "I am Orestes!" and it also stayed not.

"O," said I, "Father, these, what voices are they?"
  And even as I asked, behold the third,
  Saying: "Love those from whom ye have had evil!"

And the good Master said: "This circle scourges
  The sin of envy, and on that account
  Are drawn from love the lashes of the scourge.

The bridle of another sound shall be;
  I think that thou wilt hear it, as I judge,
  Before thou comest to the Pass of Pardon.

But fix thine eyes athwart the air right steadfast,
  And people thou wilt see before us sitting,
  And each one close against the cliff is seated."

Then wider than at first mine eyes I opened;
  I looked before me, and saw shades with mantles
  Not from the color of the stone diverse.

And when we were a little farther onward,
  I heard a cry of, "Mary, pray for us!"
  A cry of, "Michael, Peter, and all Saints!"

I do not think there walketh still on earth
  A man so hard, that he would not be pierced
  With pity at what afterward I saw.

For when I had approached so near to them
  That manifest to me their acts became,
  Drained was I at the eyes by heavy grief.

Covered with sackcloth vile they seemed to me,
  And one sustained the other with his shoulder,
  And all of them were by the bank sustained.

Thus do the blind, in want of livelihood,
  Stand at the doors of churches asking alms,
  And one upon another leans his head,

So that in others pity soon may rise,
  Not only at the accent of their words,
  But at their aspect, which no less implores.

And as unto the blind the sun comes not,
  So to the shades, of whom just now I spake,
  Heaven's light will not be bounteous of itself;

For all their lids an iron wire transpierces,
  And sews them up, as to a sparhawk wild
  Is done, because it will not quiet stay.

To me it seemed, in passing, to do outrage,
  Seeing the others without being seen;
  Wherefore I turned me to my counsel sage.

Well knew he what the mute one wished to say,
  And therefore waited not for my demand,
  But said: "Speak, and be brief, and to the point."

I had Virgilius upon that side
  Of the embankment from which one may fall,
  Since by no border 'tis engarlanded;

Upon the other side of me I had
  The shades devout, who through the horrible seam
  Pressed out the tears so that they bathed their cheeks.

To them I turned me, and, "O people, certain,"
  Began I, "of beholding the high light,
  Which your desire has solely in its care,

So may grace speedily dissolve the scum
  Upon your consciences, that limpidly
  Through them descend the river of the mind,

Tell me, for dear 'twill be to me and gracious,
  If any soul among you here is Latian,
  And 'twill perchance be good for him I learn it."

"O brother mine, each one is citizen
  Of one true city; but thy meaning is,
  Who may have lived in Italy a pilgrim."

By way of answer this I seemed to hear
  A little farther on than where I stood,
  Whereat I made myself still nearer heard.

Among the rest I saw a shade that waited
  In aspect, and should any one ask how,
  Its chin it lifted upward like a blind man.

"Spirit," I said, "who stoopest to ascend,
  If thou art he who did reply to me,
  Make thyself known to me by place or name."

"Sienese was I," it replied, "and with
  The others here recleanse my guilty life,
  Weeping to Him to lend himself to us.

Sapient I was not, although I Sapia
  Was called, and I was at another's harm
  More happy far than at my own good fortune.

And that thou mayst not think that I deceive thee,
  Hear if I was as foolish as I tell thee.
  The arc already of my years descending,

My fellow-citizens near unto Colle
  Were joined in battle with their adversaries,
  And I was praying God for what he willed.

Routed were they, and turned into the bitter
  Passes of flight; and I, the chase beholding,
  A joy received unequalled by all others;

So that I lifted upward my bold face
  Crying to God, 'Henceforth I fear thee not,'
  As did the blackbird at the little sunshine.

Peace I desired with God at the extreme
  Of my existence, and as yet would not
  My debt have been by penitence discharged,

Had it not been that in remembrance held me
  Pier Pettignano in his holy prayers,
  Who out of charity was grieved for me.

But who art thou, that into our conditions
  Questioning goest, and hast thine eyes unbound
  As I believe, and breathing dost discourse?"

"Mine eyes," I said, "will yet be here ta'en from me,
  But for short space; for small is the offence
  Committed by their being turned with envy.

Far greater is the fear, wherein suspended
  My soul is, of the torment underneath,
  For even now the load down there weighs on me."

And she to me: "Who led thee, then, among us
  Up here, if to return below thou thinkest?"
  And I: "He who is with me, and speaks not;

And living am I; therefore ask of me,
  Spirit elect, if thou wouldst have me move
  O'er yonder yet my mortal feet for thee."

"O, this is such a novel thing to hear,"
  She answered, "that great sign it is God loves thee;
  Therefore with prayer of thine sometimes assist me.

And I implore, by what thou most desirest,
  If e'er thou treadest the soil of Tuscany,
  Well with my kindred reinstate my fame.

Them wilt thou see among that people vain
  Who hope in Talamone, and will lose there
  More hope than in discovering the Diana;

But there still more the admirals will lose."

Canto XIV

"Who is this one that goes about our mountain,
  Or ever Death has given him power of flight,
  And opes his eyes and shuts them at his will?"

"I know not who, but know he's not alone;
  Ask him thyself, for thou art nearer to him,
  And gently, so that he may speak, accost him."

Thus did two spirits, leaning tow'rds each other,
  Discourse about me there on the right hand;
  Then held supine their faces to address me.

And said the one: "O soul, that, fastened still
  Within the body, tow'rds the heaven art going,
  For charity console us, and declare

Whence comest and who art thou; for thou mak'st us
  As much to marvel at this grace of thine
  As must a thing that never yet has been."

And I: "Through midst of Tuscany there wanders
  A streamlet that is born in Falterona,
  And not a hundred miles of course suffice it;

From thereupon do I this body bring.
  To tell you who I am were speech in vain,
  Because my name as yet makes no great noise."

"If well thy meaning I can penetrate
  With intellect of mine," then answered me
  He who first spake, "thou speakest of the Arno."

And said the other to him: "Why concealed
  This one the appellation of that river,
  Even as a man doth of things horrible?"

And thus the shade that questioned was of this
  Himself acquitted: "I know not; but truly
  'Tis fit the name of such a valley perish;

For from its fountain-head (where is so pregnant
  The Alpine mountain whence is cleft Peloro
  That in few places it that mark surpasses)

To where it yields itself in restoration
  Of what the heaven doth of the sea dry up,
  Whence have the rivers that which goes with them,

Virtue is like an enemy avoided
  By all, as is a serpent, through misfortune
  Of place, or through bad habit that impels them;

On which account have so transformed their nature
  The dwellers in that miserable valley,
  It seems that Circe had them in her pasture.

'Mid ugly swine, of acorns worthier
  Than other food for human use created,
  It first directeth its impoverished way.

Curs findeth it thereafter, coming downward,
  More snarling than their puissance demands,
  And turns from them disdainfully its muzzle.

It goes on falling, and the more it grows,
  The more it finds the dogs becoming wolves,
  This maledict and misadventurous ditch.

Descended then through many a hollow gulf,
  It finds the foxes so replete with fraud,
  They fear no cunning that may master them.

Nor will I cease because another hears me;
  And well 'twill be for him, if still he mind him
  Of what a truthful spirit to me unravels.

Thy grandson I behold, who doth become
  A hunter of those wolves upon the bank
  Of the wild stream, and terrifies them all.

He sells their flesh, it being yet alive;
  Thereafter slaughters them like ancient beeves;
  Many of life, himself of praise, deprives.

Blood-stained he issues from the dismal forest;
  He leaves it such, a thousand years from now
  In its primeval state 'tis not re-wooded."

As at the announcement of impending ills
  The face of him who listens is disturbed,
  From whate'er side the peril seize upon him;

So I beheld that other soul, which stood
  Turned round to listen, grow disturbed and sad,
  When it had gathered to itself the word.

The speech of one and aspect of the other
  Had me desirous made to know their names,
  And question mixed with prayers I made thereof,

Whereat the spirit which first spake to me
  Began again: "Thou wishest I should bring me
  To do for thee what thou'lt not do for me;

But since God willeth that in thee shine forth
  Such grace of his, I'll not be chary with thee;
  Know, then, that I Guido del Duca am.

My blood was so with envy set on fire,
  That if I had beheld a man make merry,
  Thou wouldst have seen me sprinkled o'er with pallor.

From my own sowing such the straw I reap!
  O human race! why dost thou set thy heart
  Where interdict of partnership must be?

This is Renier; this is the boast and honor
  Of the house of Calboli, where no one since
  Has made himself the heir of his desert.

And not alone his blood is made devoid,
  'Twixt Po and mount, and sea-shore and the Reno,
  Of good required for truth and for diversion;

For all within these boundaries is full
  Of venomous roots, so that too tardily
  By cultivation now would they diminish.

Where is good Lizio, and Arrigo Manardi,
  Pier Traversaro, and Guido di Carpigna,
  O Romagnuoli into bastards turned?

When in Bologna will a Fabbro rise?
  When in Faenza a Bernardin di Fosco,
  The noble scion of ignoble seed?

Be not astonished, Tuscan, if I weep,
  When I remember, with Guido da Prata,
  Ugolin d' Azzo, who was living with us,

Frederick Tignoso and his company,
  The house of Traversara, and th' Anastagi,
  And one race and the other is extinct;

The dames and cavaliers, the toils and ease
  That filled our souls with love and courtesy,
  There where the hearts have so malicious grown!

O Brettinoro! why dost thou not flee,
  Seeing that all thy family is gone,
  And many people, not to be corrupted?

Bagnacaval does well in not begetting
  And ill does Castrocaro, and Conio worse,
  In taking trouble to beget such Counts.

Will do well the Pagani, when their Devil
  Shall have departed; but not therefore pure
  Will testimony of them e'er remain.

O Ugolin de' Fantoli, secure
  Thy name is, since no longer is awaited
  One who, degenerating, can obscure it!

But go now, Tuscan, for it now delights me
  To weep far better than it does to speak,
  So much has our discourse my mind distressed."

We were aware that those beloved souls
  Heard us depart; therefore, by keeping silent,
  They made us of our pathway confident.

When we became alone by going onward,
  Thunder, when it doth cleave the air, appeared
  A voice, that counter to us came, exclaiming:

"Shall slay me whosoever findeth me!"
  And fled as the reverberation dies
  If suddenly the cloud asunder bursts.

As soon as hearing had a truce from this,
  Behold another, with so great a crash,
  That it resembled thunderings following fast:

"I am Aglaurus, who became a stone!"
  And then, to press myself close to the Poet,
  I backward, and not forward, took a step.

Already on all sides the air was quiet;
  And said he to me: "That was the hard curb
  That ought to hold a man within his bounds;

But you take in the bait so that the hook
  Of the old Adversary draws you to him,
  And hence availeth little curb or call.

The heavens are calling you, and wheel around you,
  Displaying to you their eternal beauties,
  And still your eye is looking on the ground;

Whence He, who all discerns, chastises you."

Canto XV

As much as 'twixt the close of the third hour
  And dawn of day appeareth of that sphere
  Which aye in fashion of a child is playing,

So much it now appeared, towards the night,
  Was of his course remaining to the sun;
  There it was evening, and 'twas midnight here;

And the rays smote the middle of our faces,
  Because by us the mount was so encircled,
  That straight towards the west we now were going

When I perceived my forehead overpowered
  Beneath the splendor far more than at first,
  And stupor were to me the things unknown,

Whereat towards the summit of my brow
  I raised my hands, and made myself the visor
  Which the excessive glare diminishes.

As when from off the water, or a mirror,
  The sunbeam leaps unto the opposite side,
  Ascending upward in the selfsame measure

That it descends, and deviates as far
  From falling of a stone in line direct,
  (As demonstrate experiment and art,)

So it appeared to me that by a light
  Refracted there before me I was smitten;
  On which account my sight was swift to flee.

"What is that, Father sweet, from which I cannot
  So fully screen my sight that it avail me,"
  Said I, "and seems towards us to be moving?"

"Marvel thou not, if dazzle thee as yet
  The family of heaven," he answered me;
  "An angel 'tis, who comes to invite us upward.

Soon will it be, that to behold these things
  Shall not be grievous, but delightful to thee
  As much as nature fashioned thee to feel."

When we had reached the Angel benedight,
  With joyful voice he said: "Here enter in
  To stairway far less steep than are the others."

We mounting were, already thence departed,
  And "Beati misericordes" was
  Behind us sung, "Rejoice, thou that o'ercomest!"

My Master and myself, we two alone
  Were going upward, and I thought, in going,
  Some profit to acquire from words of his;

And I to him directed me, thus asking:
  "What did the spirit of Romagna mean,
  Mentioning interdict and partnership?"

Whence he to me: "Of his own greatest failing
  He knows the harm; and therefore wonder not
  If he reprove us, that we less may rue it.

Because are thither pointed your desires
  Where by companionship each share is lessened,
  Envy doth ply the bellows to your sighs.

But if the love of the supernal sphere
  Should upwardly direct your aspiration,
  There would not be that fear within your breast;

For there, as much the more as one says 'Our,'
  So much the more of good each one possesses,
  And more of charity in that cloister burns."

"I am more hungering to be satisfied,"
  I said, "than if I had before been silent,
  And more of doubt within my mind I gather.

How can it be, that boon distributed
  The more possessors can more wealthy make
  Therein, than if by few it be possessed?"

And he to me: "Because thou fixest still
  Thy mind entirely upon earthly things,
  Thou pluckest darkness from the very light.

That goodness infinite and ineffable
  Which is above there, runneth unto love,
  As to a lucid body comes the sunbeam.

So much it gives itself as it finds ardour,
  So that as far as charity extends,
  O'er it increases the eternal valour.

And the more people thitherward aspire,
  More are there to love well, and more they love there,
  And, as a mirror, one reflects the other.

And if my reasoning appease thee not,
  Thou shalt see Beatrice; and she will fully
  Take from thee this and every other longing.

Endeavour, then, that soon may be extinct,
  As are the two already, the five wounds
  That close themselves again by being painful."

Even as I wished to say, "Thou dost appease me,"
  I saw that I had reached another circle,
  So that my eager eyes made me keep silence.

There it appeared to me that in a vision
  Ecstatic on a sudden I was rapt,
  And in a temple many persons saw;

And at the door a woman, with the sweet
  Behaviour of a mother, saying: "Son,
  Why in this manner hast thou dealt with us?

Lo, sorrowing, thy father and myself
  Were seeking for thee;"—and as here she ceased,
  That which appeared at first had disappeared.

Then I beheld another with those waters
  Adown her cheeks which grief distils whenever
  From great disdain of others it is born,

And saying: "If of that city thou art lord,
  For whose name was such strife among the gods,
  And whence doth every science scintillate,

Avenge thyself on those audacious arms
  That clasped our daughter, O Pisistratus;"
  And the lord seemed to me benign and mild

To answer her with aspect temperate:
  "What shall we do to those who wish us ill,
  If he who loves us be by us condemned?"

Then saw I people hot in fire of wrath,
  With stones a young man slaying, clamorously
  Still crying to each other, "Kill him! kill him!"

And him I saw bow down, because of death
  That weighed already on him, to the earth,
  But of his eyes made ever gates to heaven,

Imploring the high Lord, in so great strife,
  That he would pardon those his persecutors,
  With such an aspect as unlocks compassion.

Soon as my soul had outwardly returned
  To things external to it which are true,
  Did I my not false errors recognize.

My Leader, who could see me bear myself
  Like to a man that rouses him from sleep,
  Exclaimed: "What ails thee, that thou canst not stand?

But hast been coming more than half a league
  Veiling thine eyes, and with thy legs entangled,
  In guise of one whom wine or sleep subdues?"

"O my sweet Father, if thou listen to me,
  I'll tell thee," said I, "what appeared to me,
  When thus from me my legs were ta'en away."

And he: "If thou shouldst have a hundred masks
  Upon thy face, from me would not be shut
  Thy cogitations, howsoever small.

What thou hast seen was that thou mayst not fail
  To ope thy heart unto the waters of peace,
  Which from the eternal fountain are diffused.

I did not ask, 'What ails thee?' as he does
  Who only looketh with the eyes that see not
  When of the soul bereft the body lies,

But asked it to give vigour to thy feet;
  Thus must we needs urge on the sluggards, slow
  To use their wakefulness when it returns."

We passed along, athwart the twilight peering
  Forward as far as ever eye could stretch
  Against the sunbeams serotine and lucent;

And lo! by slow degrees a smoke approached
  In our direction, sombre as the night,
  Nor was there place to hide one's self therefrom.

This of our eyes and the pure air bereft us.

Canto XVI

Darkness of hell, and of a night deprived
  Of every planet under a poor sky,
  As much as may be tenebrous with cloud,

Ne'er made unto my sight so thick a veil,
  As did that smoke which there enveloped us,
  Nor to the feeling of so rough a texture;

For not an eye it suffered to stay open;
  Whereat mine escort, faithful and sagacious,
  Drew near to me and offered me his shoulder.

E'en as a blind man goes behind his guide,
  Lest he should wander, or should strike against
  Aught that may harm or peradventure kill him,

So went I through the bitter and foul air,
  Listening unto my Leader, who said only,
  "Look that from me thou be not separated."

Voices I heard, and every one appeared
  To supplicate for peace and misericord
  The Lamb of God who takes away our sins.

Still "Agnus Dei" their exordium was;
  One word there was in all, and metre one,
  So that all harmony appeared among them.

"Master," I said, "are spirits those I hear?"
  And he to me: "Thou apprehendest truly,
  And they the knot of anger go unloosing."

"Now who art thou, that cleavest through our smoke
  And art discoursing of us even as though
  Thou didst by calends still divide the time?"

After this manner by a voice was spoken;
  Whereon my Master said: "Do thou reply,
  And ask if on this side the way go upward."

And I: "O creature that dost cleanse thyself
  To return beautiful to Him who made thee,
  Thou shalt hear marvels if thou follow me."

"Thee will I follow far as is allowed me,"
  He answered; "and if smoke prevent our seeing,
  Hearing shall keep us joined instead thereof."

Thereon began I: "With that swathing band
  Which death unwindeth am I going upward,
  And hither came I through the infernal anguish.

And if God in his grace has me infolded,
  So that he wills that I behold his court
  By method wholly out of modern usage,

Conceal not from me who ere death thou wast,
  But tell it me, and tell me if I go
  Right for the pass, and be thy words our escort."

"Lombard was I, and I was Marco called;
  The world I knew, and loved that excellence,
  At which has each one now unbent his bow.

For mounting upward, thou art going right."
  Thus he made answer, and subjoined: "I pray thee
  To pray for me when thou shalt be above."

And I to him: "My faith I pledge to thee
  To do what thou dost ask me; but am bursting
  Inly with doubt, unless I rid me of it.

First it was simple, and is now made double
  By thy opinion, which makes certain to me,
  Here and elsewhere, that which I couple with it.

The world forsooth is utterly deserted
  By every virtue, as thou tellest me,
  And with iniquity is big and covered;

But I beseech thee point me out the cause,
  That I may see it, and to others show it;
  For one in the heavens, and here below one puts it."

A sigh profound, that grief forced into Ai!
  He first sent forth, and then began he: "Brother,
  The world is blind, and sooth thou comest from it!

Ye who are living every cause refer
  Still upward to the heavens, as if all things
  They of necessity moved with themselves.

If this were so, in you would be destroyed
  Free will, nor any justice would there be
  In having joy for good, or grief for evil.

The heavens your movements do initiate,
  I say not all; but granting that I say it,
  Light has been given you for good and evil,

And free volition; which, if some fatigue
  In the first battles with the heavens it suffers,
  Afterwards conquers all, if well 'tis nurtured.

To greater force and to a better nature,
  Though free, ye subject are, and that creates
  The mind in you the heavens have not in charge.

Hence, if the present world doth go astray,
In you the cause is, be it sought in you;
And I therein will now be thy true spy.

Forth from the hand of Him, who fondles it
Before it is, like to a little girl
Weeping and laughing in her childish sport,

Issues the simple soul, that nothing knows,
Save that, proceeding from a joyous Maker,
Gladly it turns to that which gives it pleasure.

Of trivial good at first it tastes the savour;
Is cheated by it, and runs after it,
If guide or rein turn not aside its love.

Hence it behoved laws for a rein to place,
Behoved a king to have, who at the least
Of the true city should discern the tower.

The laws exist, but who sets hand to them?
No one; because the shepherd who precedes
Can ruminate, but cleaveth not the hoof;

Wherefore the people that perceives its guide
Strike only at the good for which it hankers,
Feeds upon that, and farther seeketh not.

Clearly canst thou perceive that evil guidance
The cause is that has made the world depraved,
And not that nature is corrupt in you.

Rome, that reformed the world, accustomed was
Two suns to have, which one road and the other,
Of God and of the world, made manifest.

One has the other quenched, and to the crosier
The sword is joined, and ill beseemeth it
That by main force one with the other go,

Because, being joined, one feareth not the other;
If thou believe not, think upon the grain,
For by its seed each herb is recognized.

In the land laved by Po and Adige,
  Valour and courtesy used to be found,
  Before that Frederick had his controversy;

Now in security can pass that way
  Whoever will abstain, through sense of shame,
  From speaking with the good, or drawing near them.

True, three old men are left, in whom upbraids
  The ancient age the new, and late they deem it
  That God restore them to the better life:

Currado da Palazzo, and good Gherardo,
  And Guido da Castel, who better named is,
  In fashion of the French, the simple Lombard:

Say thou henceforward that the Church of Rome,
  Confounding in itself two governments,
  Falls in the mire, and soils itself and burden."

"O Marco mine," I said, "thou reasonest well;
  And now discern I why the sons of Levi
  Have been excluded from the heritage.

But what Gherardo is it, who, as sample
  Of a lost race, thou sayest has remained
  In reprobation of the barbarous age?"

"Either thy speech deceives me, or it tempts me,"
  He answered me; "for speaking Tuscan to me,
  It seems of good Gherardo naught thou knowest.

By other surname do I know him not,
  Unless I take it from his daughter Gaia.
  May God be with you, for I come no farther.

Behold the dawn, that through the smoke rays out,
  Already whitening; and I must depart—
  Yonder the Angel is—ere he appear."

Thus did he speak, and would no farther hear me.

Canto XVII

Remember, Reader, if e'er in the Alps
  A mist o'ertook thee, through which thou couldst see
  Not otherwise than through its membrane mole,

How, when the vapours humid and condensed
  Begin to dissipate themselves, the sphere
  Of the sun feebly enters in among them,

And thy imagination will be swift
  In coming to perceive how I re-saw
  The sun at first, that was already setting.

Thus, to the faithful footsteps of my Master
  Mating mine own, I issued from that cloud
  To rays already dead on the low shores.

O thou, Imagination, that dost steal us
  So from without sometimes, that man perceives not,
  Although around may sound a thousand trumpets,

Who moveth thee, if sense impel thee not?
  Moves thee a light, which in the heaven takes form,
  By self, or by a will that downward guides it.

Of her impiety, who changed her form
  Into the bird that most delights in singing,
  In my imagining appeared the trace;

And hereupon my mind was so withdrawn
  Within itself, that from without there came
  Nothing that then might be received by it.

Then reigned within my lofty fantasy
  One crucified, disdainful and ferocious
  In countenance, and even thus was dying.

Around him were the great Ahasuerus,
  Esther his wife, and the just Mordecai,
  Who was in word and action so entire.

And even as this image burst asunder
  Of its own self, in fashion of a bubble
  In which the water it was made of fails,

There rose up in my vision a young maiden
  Bitterly weeping, and she said: "O queen,
  Why hast thou wished in anger to be naught?

Thou'st slain thyself, Lavinia not to lose;
  Now hast thou lost me; I am she who mourns,
  Mother, at thine ere at another's ruin."

As sleep is broken, when upon a sudden
  New light strikes in upon the eyelids closed,
  And broken quivers ere it dieth wholly,

So this imagining of mine fell down
  As soon as the effulgence smote my face,
  Greater by far than what is in our wont.

I turned me round to see where I might be,
  When said a voice, "Here is the passage up;"
  Which from all other purposes removed me,

And made my wish so full of eagerness
  To look and see who was it that was speaking,
  It never rests till meeting face to face;

But as before the sun, which quells the sight,
  And in its own excess its figure veils,
  Even so my power was insufficient here.

"This is a spirit divine, who in the way
  Of going up directs us without asking,
  And who with his own light himself conceals.

He does with us as man doth with himself;
  For he who sees the need, and waits the asking,
  Malignly leans already tow'rds denial.

Accord we now our feet to such inviting,
  Let us make haste to mount ere it grow dark;
  For then we could not till the day return."

Thus my Conductor said; and I and he
  Together turned our footsteps to a stairway;
  And I, as soon as the first step I reached,

Near me perceived a motion as of wings,
  And fanning in the face, and saying, "'Beati
  Pacifici,' who are without ill anger."

Already over us were so uplifted
  The latest sunbeams, which the night pursues,
  That upon many sides the stars appeared.

"O manhood mine, why dost thou vanish so?"
  I said within myself; for I perceived
  The vigour of my legs was put in truce.

We at the point were where no more ascends
  The stairway upward, and were motionless,
  Even as a ship, which at the shore arrives;

And I gave heed a little, if I might hear
  Aught whatsoever in the circle new;
  Then to my Master turned me round and said:

"Say, my sweet Father, what delinquency
  Is purged here in the circle where we are?
  Although our feet may pause, pause not thy speech."

And he to me: "The love of good, remiss
  In what it should have done, is here restored;
  Here plied again the ill-belated oar;

But still more openly to understand,
  Turn unto me thy mind, and thou shalt gather
  Some profitable fruit from our delay.

Neither Creator nor a creature ever,
  Son," he began, "was destitute of love
  Natural or spiritual; and thou knowest it.

The natural was ever without error;
  But err the other may by evil object,
  Or by too much, or by too little vigour.

While in the first it well directed is,
  And in the second moderates itself,
  It cannot be the cause of sinful pleasure;

But when to ill it turns, and, with more care
  Or lesser than it ought, runs after good,
  'Gainst the Creator works his own creation.

Hence thou mayst comprehend that love must be
  The seed within yourselves of every virtue,
  And every act that merits punishment.

Now inasmuch as never from the welfare
  Of its own subject can love turn its sight,
  From their own hatred all things are secure;

And since we cannot think of any being
  Standing alone, nor from the First divided,
  Of hating Him is all desire cut off.

Hence if, discriminating, I judge well,
  The evil that one loves is of one's neighbor,
  And this is born in three modes in your clay.

There are, who, by abasement of their neighbor,
  Hope to excel, and therefore only long
  That from his greatness he may be cast down;

There are, who power, grace, honor, and renown
  Fear they may lose because another rises,
  Thence are so sad that the reverse they love;

And there are those whom injury seems to chafe,
  So that it makes them greedy for revenge,
  And such must needs shape out another's harm.

This threefold love is wept for down below;
  Now of the other will I have thee hear,
  That runneth after good with measure faulty.

Each one confusedly a good conceives
  Wherein the mind may rest, and longeth for it;
  Therefore to overtake it each one strives.

If languid love to look on this attract you,
  Or in attaining unto it, this cornice,
  After just penitence, torments you for it.

There's other good that does not make man happy;
  'Tis not felicity, 'tis not the good
  Essence, of every good the fruit and root.

The love that yields itself too much to this
  Above us is lamented in three circles;
  But how tripartite it may be described,

I say not, that thou seek it for thyself."

Canto XVIII

An end had put unto his reasoning
  The lofty Teacher, and attent was looking
  Into my face, if I appeared content;

And I, whom a new thirst still goaded on,
  Without was mute, and said within: "Perchance
  The too much questioning I make annoys him."

But that true Father, who had comprehended
  The timid wish, that opened not itself,
  By speaking gave me hardihood to speak.

Whence I: "My sight is, Master, vivified
  So in thy light, that clearly I discern
  Whate'er thy speech importeth or describes.

Therefore I thee entreat, sweet Father dear,
  To teach me love, to which thou dost refer
  Every good action and its contrary."

"Direct," he said, "towards me the keen eyes
  Of intellect, and clear will be to thee
  The error of the blind, who would be leaders.

The soul, which is created apt to love,
  Is mobile unto everything that pleases,
  Soon as by pleasure she is waked to action.

Your apprehension from some real thing
  An image draws, and in yourselves displays it
  So that it makes the soul turn unto it.

And if, when turned, towards it she incline,
  Love is that inclination; it is nature,
  Which is by pleasure bound in you anew

Then even as the fire doth upward move
  By its own form, which to ascend is born,
  Where longest in its matter it endures,

So comes the captive soul into desire,
  Which is a motion spiritual, and ne'er rests
  Until she doth enjoy the thing beloved.

Now may apparent be to thee how hidden
  The truth is from those people, who aver
  All love is in itself a laudable thing;

Because its matter may perchance appear
  Aye to be good; but yet not each impression
  Is good, albeit good may be the wax."

"Thy words, and my sequacious intellect,"
  I answered him, "have love revealed to me;
  But that has made me more impregned with doubt;

For if love from without be offered us,
  And with another foot the soul go not,
  If right or wrong she go, 'tis not her merit."

And he to me: "What reason seeth here,
  Myself can tell thee; beyond that await
  For Beatrice, since 'tis a work of faith.

Every substantial form, that segregate
  From matter is, and with it is united,
  Specific power has in itself collected,

Which without act is not perceptible,
  Nor shows itself except by its effect,
  As life does in a plant by the green leaves.

But still, whence cometh the intelligence
Of the first notions, man is ignorant,
And the affection for the first allurements,

Which are in you as instinct in the bee
To make its honey; and this first desire
Merit of praise or blame containeth not.

Now, that to this all others may be gathered,
Innate within you is the power that counsels,
And it should keep the threshold of assent.

This is the principle, from which is taken
Occasion of desert in you, according
As good and guilty loves it takes and winnows.

Those who, in reasoning, to the bottom went,
Were of this innate liberty aware,
Therefore bequeathed they Ethics to the world.

Supposing, then, that from necessity
Springs every love that is within you kindled,
Within yourselves the power is to restrain it.

The noble virtue Beatrice understands
By the free will; and therefore see that thou
Bear it in mind, if she should speak of it."

The moon, belated almost unto midnight,
Now made the stars appear to us more rare,
Formed like a bucket, that is all ablaze,

And counter to the heavens ran through those paths
Which the sun sets aflame, when he of Rome
Sees it 'twixt Sardes and Corsicans go down;

And that patrician shade, for whom is named
Pietola more than any Mantuan town,
Had laid aside the burden of my lading;

Whence I, who reason manifest and plain
In answer to my questions had received,
Stood like a man in drowsy reverie.

But taken from me was this drowsiness
  Suddenly by a people, that behind
  Our backs already had come round to us.

And as, of old, Ismenus and Asopus
  Beside them saw at night the rush and throng,
  If but the Thebans were in need of Bacchus,

So they along that circle curve their step,
  From what I saw of those approaching us,
  Who by good-will and righteous love are ridden.

Full soon they were upon us, because running
  Moved onward all that mighty multitude,
  And two in the advance cried out, lamenting,

"Mary in haste unto the mountain ran,
  And Caesar, that he might subdue Ilerda,
  Thrust at Marseilles, and then ran into Spain."

"Quick! quick! so that the time may not be lost
  By little love!" forthwith the others cried,
  "For ardour in well-doing freshens grace!"

"O folk, in whom an eager fervour now
  Supplies perhaps delay and negligence,
  Put by you in well-doing, through lukewarmness,

This one who lives, and truly I lie not,
  Would fain go up, if but the sun relight us;
  So tell us where the passage nearest is."

These were the words of him who was my Guide;
  And some one of those spirits said: "Come on
  Behind us, and the opening shalt thou find;

So full of longing are we to move onward,
  That stay we cannot; therefore pardon us,
  If thou for churlishness our justice take.

I was San Zeno's Abbot at Verona,
  Under the empire of good Barbarossa,
  Of whom still sorrowing Milan holds discourse;

And he has one foot in the grave already,
  Who shall erelong lament that monastery,
  And sorry be of having there had power,

Because his son, in his whole body sick,
  And worse in mind, and who was evil-born,
  He put into the place of its true pastor."

If more he said, or silent was, I know not,
  He had already passed so far beyond us;
  But this I heard, and to retain it pleased me.

And he who was in every need my succor
  Said: "Turn thee hitherward; see two of them
  Come fastening upon slothfulness their teeth."

In rear of all they shouted: "Sooner were
  The people dead to whom the sea was opened,
  Than their inheritors the Jordan saw;

And those who the fatigue did not endure
  Unto the issue, with Anchises' son,
  Themselves to life withouten glory offered."

Then when from us so separated were
  Those shades, that they no longer could be seen,
  Within me a new thought did entrance find,

Whence others many and diverse were born;
  And so I lapsed from one into another,
  That in a reverie mine eyes I closed,

And meditation into dream transmuted.

Canto XIX

It was the hour when the diurnal heat
  No more can warm the coldness of the moon,
  Vanquished by earth, or peradventure Saturn,

When geomancers their Fortuna Major
  See in the orient before the dawn
  Rise by a path that long remains not dim,

There came to me in dreams a stammering woman,
  Squint in her eyes, and in her feet distorted,
  With hands dissevered and of sallow hue.

I looked at her; and as the sun restores
  The frigid members which the night benumbs,
  Even thus my gaze did render voluble

Her tongue, and made her all erect thereafter
  In little while, and the lost countenance
  As love desires it so in her did color.

When in this wise she had her speech unloosed,
  She 'gan to sing so, that with difficulty
  Could I have turned my thoughts away from her.

"I am," she sang, "I am the Siren sweet
  Who mariners amid the main unman,
  So full am I of pleasantness to hear.

I drew Ulysses from his wandering way
  Unto my song, and he who dwells with me
  Seldom departs so wholly I content him."

Her mouth was not yet closed again, before
  Appeared a Lady saintly and alert
  Close at my side to put her to confusion.

"Virgilius, O Virgilius! who is this?"
  Sternly she said; and he was drawing near
  With eyes still fixed upon that modest one.

She seized the other and in front laid open,
  Rending her garments, and her belly showed me;
  This waked me with the stench that issued from it.

I turned mine eyes, and good Virgilius said:
  "At least thrice have I called thee; rise and come;
  Find we the opening by which thou mayst enter."

I rose; and full already of high day
  Were all the circles of the Sacred Mountain,
  And with the new sun at our back we went.

Following behind him, I my forehead bore
  Like unto one who has it laden with thought,
  Who makes himself the half arch of a bridge,

When I heard say, "Come, here the passage is,"
  Spoken in a manner gentle and benign,
  Such as we hear not in this mortal region.

With open wings, which of a swan appeared,
  Upward he turned us who thus spake to us,
  Between the two walls of the solid granite.

He moved his pinions afterwards and fanned us,
  Affirming those 'qui lugent' to be blessed,
  For they shall have their souls with comfort filled.

"What aileth thee, that aye to earth thou gazest?"
  To me my Guide began to say, we both
  Somewhat beyond the Angel having mounted.

And I: "With such misgiving makes me go
  A vision new, which bends me to itself,
  So that I cannot from the thought withdraw me."

"Didst thou behold," he said, "that old enchantress,
  Who sole above us henceforth is lamented?
  Didst thou behold how man is freed from her?

Suffice it thee, and smite earth with thy heels,
  Thine eyes lift upward to the lure, that whirls
  The Eternal King with revolutions vast."

Even as the hawk, that first his feet surveys,
  Then turns him to the call and stretches forward,
  Through the desire of food that draws him thither,

Such I became, and such, as far as cleaves
  The rock to give a way to him who mounts,
  Went on to where the circling doth begin.

On the fifth circle when I had come forth,
  People I saw upon it who were weeping,
  Stretched prone upon the ground, all downward turned.

"Adhaesit pavimento anima mea,"
  I heard them say with sighings so profound,
  That hardly could the words be understood.

"O ye elect of God, whose sufferings
  Justice and Hope both render less severe,
  Direct ye us towards the high ascents."

"If ye are come secure from this prostration,
  And wish to find the way most speedily,
  Let your right hands be evermore outside."

Thus did the Poet ask, and thus was answered
  By them somewhat in front of us; whence I
  In what was spoken divined the rest concealed,

And unto my Lord's eyes mine eyes I turned;
  Whence he assented with a cheerful sign
  To what the sight of my desire implored.

When of myself I could dispose at will,
  Above that creature did I draw myself,
  Whose words before had caused me to take note,

Saying: "O Spirit, in whom weeping ripens
  That without which to God we cannot turn,
  Suspend awhile for me thy greater care.

Who wast thou, and why are your backs turned upwards,
  Tell me, and if thou wouldst that I procure thee
  Anything there whence living I departed."

And he to me: "Wherefore our backs the heaven
  Turns to itself, know shalt thou; but beforehand
  'Scias quod ego fui successor Petri.'

Between Siestri and Chiaveri descends
  A river beautiful, and of its name
  The title of my blood its summit makes.

A month and little more essayed I how
  Weighs the great cloak on him from mire who keeps it,
  For all the other burdens seem a feather.

Tardy, ah woe is me! was my conversion;
  But when the Roman Shepherd I was made,
  Then I discovered life to be a lie.

I saw that there the heart was not at rest,
  Nor farther in that life could one ascend;
  Whereby the love of this was kindled in me.

Until that time a wretched soul and parted
  From God was I, and wholly avaricious;
  Now, as thou seest, I here am punished for it.

What avarice does is here made manifest
  In the purgation of these souls converted,
  And no more bitter pain the Mountain has.

Even as our eye did not uplift itself
  Aloft, being fastened upon earthly things,
  So justice here has merged it in the earth.

As avarice had extinguished our affection
  For every good, whereby was action lost,
  So justice here doth hold us in restraint,

Bound and imprisoned by the feet and hands;
  And so long as it pleases the just Lord
  Shall we remain immovable and prostrate."

I on my knees had fallen, and wished to speak;
  But even as I began, and he was 'ware,
  Only by listening, of my reverence,

"What cause," he said, "has downward bent thee thus?"
  And I to him: "For your own dignity,
  Standing, my conscience stung me with remorse."

"Straighten thy legs, and upward raise thee, brother,"
  He answered: "Err not, fellow-servant am I
  With thee and with the others to one power.

If e'er that holy, evangelic sound,
  Which sayeth 'neque nubent,' thou hast heard,
  Well canst thou see why in this wise I speak.

Now go; no longer will I have thee linger,
  Because thy stay doth incommode my weeping,
  With which I ripen that which thou hast said.

On earth I have a grandchild named Alagia,
  Good in herself, unless indeed our house
  Malevolent may make her by example,

And she alone remains to me on earth."

Canto XX

Ill strives the will against a better will;
  Therefore, to pleasure him, against my pleasure
  I drew the sponge not saturate from the water.

Onward I moved, and onward moved my Leader,
  Through vacant places, skirting still the rock,
  As on a wall close to the battlements;

For they that through their eyes pour drop by drop
  The malady which all the world pervades,
  On the other side too near the verge approach.

Accursed mayst thou be, thou old she-wolf,
  That more than all the other beasts hast prey,
  Because of hunger infinitely hollow!

O heaven, in whose gyrations some appear
  To think conditions here below are changed,
  When will he come through whom she shall depart?

Onward we went with footsteps slow and scarce,
  And I attentive to the shades I heard
  Piteously weeping and bemoaning them;

And I by peradventure heard "Sweet Mary!"
  Uttered in front of us amid the weeping
  Even as a woman does who is in child-birth;

And in continuance: "How poor thou wast
  Is manifested by that hostelry
  Where thou didst lay thy sacred burden down."

Thereafterward I heard: "O good Fabricius,
  Virtue with poverty didst thou prefer
  To the possession of great wealth with vice."

So pleasurable were these words to me
  That I drew farther onward to have knowledge
  Touching that spirit whence they seemed to come.

He furthermore was speaking of the largess
  Which Nicholas unto the maidens gave,
  In order to conduct their youth to honor.

"O soul that dost so excellently speak,
  Tell me who wast thou," said I, "and why only
  Thou dost renew these praises well deserved?

Not without recompense shall be thy word,
  If I return to finish the short journey
  Of that life which is flying to its end."

And he: "I'll tell thee, not for any comfort
  I may expect from earth, but that so much
  Grace shines in thee or ever thou art dead.

I was the root of that malignant plant
  Which overshadows all the Christian world,
  So that good fruit is seldom gathered from it;

But if Douay and Ghent, and Lille and Bruges
  Had Power, soon vengeance would be taken on it;
  And this I pray of Him who judges all.

Hugh Capet was I called upon the earth;
  From me were born the Louises and Philips,
  By whom in later days has France been governed.

I was the son of a Parisian butcher,
  What time the ancient kings had perished all,
  Excepting one, contrite in cloth of gray.

I found me grasping in my hands the rein
  Of the realm's government, and so great power
  Of new acquest, and so with friends abounding,

That to the widowed diadem promoted
  The head of mine own offspring was, from whom
  The consecrated bones of these began.

So long as the great dowry of Provence
  Out of my blood took not the sense of shame,
  'Twas little worth, but still it did no harm.

Then it began with falsehood and with force
  Its rapine; and thereafter, for amends,
  Took Ponthieu, Normandy, and Gascony.

Charles came to Italy, and for amends
  A victim made of Conradin, and then
  Thrust Thomas back to heaven, for amends.

A time I see, not very distant now,
  Which draweth forth another Charles from France,
  The better to make known both him and his.

Unarmed he goes, and only with the lance
  That Judas jousted with; and that he thrusts
  So that he makes the paunch of Florence burst.

He thence not land, but sin and infamy,
  Shall gain, so much more grievous to himself
  As the more light such damage he accounts.

The other, now gone forth, ta'en in his ship,
  See I his daughter sell, and chaffer for her
  As corsairs do with other female slaves.

What more, O Avarice, canst thou do to us,
  Since thou my blood so to thyself hast drawn,
  It careth not for its own proper flesh?

That less may seem the future ill and past,
  I see the flower-de-luce Alagna enter,
  And Christ in his own Vicar captive made.

I see him yet another time derided;
  I see renewed the vinegar and gall,
  And between living thieves I see him slain.

I see the modern Pilate so relentless,
  This does not sate him, but without decretal
  He to the temple bears his sordid sails!

When, O my Lord! shall I be joyful made
  By looking on the vengeance which, concealed,
  Makes sweet thine anger in thy secrecy?

What I was saying of that only bride
  Of the Holy Ghost, and which occasioned thee
  To turn towards me for some commentary,

So long has been ordained to all our prayers
  As the day lasts; but when the night comes on,
  Contrary sound we take instead thereof.

At that time we repeat Pygmalion,
  Of whom a traitor, thief, and parricide
  Made his insatiable desire of gold;

And the misery of avaricious Midas,
  That followed his inordinate demand,
  At which forevermore one needs but laugh.

The foolish Achan each one then records,
  And how he stole the spoils; so that the wrath
  Of Joshua still appears to sting him here.

Then we accuse Sapphira with her husband,
  We laud the hoof-beats Heliodorus had,
  And the whole mount in infamy encircles

Polymnestor who murdered Polydorus.
  Here finally is cried: 'O Crassus, tell us,
  For thou dost know, what is the taste of gold?'

Sometimes we speak, one loud, another low,
  According to desire of speech, that spurs us
  To greater now and now to lesser pace.

But in the good that here by day is talked of,
  Erewhile alone I was not; yet near by
  No other person lifted up his voice."

From him already we departed were,
  And made endeavour to o'ercome the road
  As much as was permitted to our power,

When I perceived, like something that is falling,
  The mountain tremble, whence a chill seized on me,
  As seizes him who to his death is going.

Certes so violently shook not Delos,
  Before Latona made her nest therein
  To give birth to the two eyes of the heaven.

Then upon all sides there began a cry,
  Such that the Master drew himself towards me,
  Saying, "Fear not, while I am guiding thee."

"Gloria in excelsis Deo," all
  Were saying, from what near I comprehended,
  Where it was possible to hear the cry.

We paused immovable and in suspense,
  Even as the shepherds who first heard that song,
  Until the trembling ceased, and it was finished.

Then we resumed again our holy path,
  Watching the shades that lay upon the ground,
  Already turned to their accustomed plaint.

No ignorance ever with so great a strife
  Had rendered me importunate to know,
  If erreth not in this my memory,

As meditating then I seemed to have;
  Nor out of haste to question did I dare,
  Nor of myself I there could aught perceive;

So I went onward timorous and thoughtful.

Canto XXI

The natural thirst, that ne'er is satisfied
  Excepting with the water for whose grace
  The woman of Samaria besought,

Put me in travail, and haste goaded me
　Along the encumbered path behind my Leader
　And I was pitying that righteous vengeance;

And lo! in the same manner as Luke writeth
　That Christ appeared to two upon the way
　From the sepulchral cave already risen,

A shade appeared to us, and came behind us,
　Down gazing on the prostrate multitude,
　Nor were we ware of it, until it spake,

Saying, "My brothers, may God give you peace!"
　We turned us suddenly, and Virgilius rendered
　To him the countersign thereto conforming.

Thereon began he: "In the blessed council,
　Thee may the court veracious place in peace,
　That me doth banish in eternal exile!"

"How," said he, and the while we went with speed,
　"If ye are shades whom God deigns not on high,
　Who up his stairs so far has guided you?"

And said my Teacher: "If thou note the marks
　Which this one bears, and which the Angel traces
　Well shalt thou see he with the good must reign.

But because she who spinneth day and night
　For him had not yet drawn the distaff off,
　Which Clotho lays for each one and compacts,

His soul, which is thy sister and my own,
　In coming upwards could not come alone,
　By reason that it sees not in our fashion.

Whence I was drawn from out the ample throat
　Of Hell to be his guide, and I shall guide him
　As far on as my school has power to lead.

But tell us, if thou knowest, why such a shudder
　Erewhile the mountain gave, and why together
　All seemed to cry, as far as its moist feet?"

In asking he so hit the very eye
  Of my desire, that merely with the hope
  My thirst became the less unsatisfied.

"Naught is there," he began, "that without order
  May the religion of the mountain feel,
  Nor aught that may be foreign to its custom.

Free is it here from every permutation;
  What from itself heaven in itself receiveth
  Can be of this the cause, and naught beside;

Because that neither rain, nor hail, nor snow,
  Nor dew, nor hoar-frost any higher falls
  Than the short, little stairway of three steps.

Dense clouds do not appear, nor rarefied,
  Nor coruscation, nor the daughter of Thaumas,
  That often upon earth her region shifts;

No arid vapour any farther rises
  Than to the top of the three steps I spake of,
  Whereon the Vicar of Peter has his feet.

Lower down perchance it trembles less or more,
  But, for the wind that in the earth is hidden
  I know not how, up here it never trembled.

It trembles here, whenever any soul
  Feels itself pure, so that it soars, or moves
  To mount aloft, and such a cry attends it.

Of purity the will alone gives proof,
  Which, being wholly free to change its convent,
  Takes by surprise the soul, and helps it fly.

First it wills well; but the desire permits not,
  Which divine justice with the self-same will
  There was to sin, upon the torment sets.

And I, who have been lying in this pain
  Five hundred years and more, but just now felt
  A free volition for a better seat.

Therefore thou heardst the earthquake, and the pious
  Spirits along the mountain rendering praise
  Unto the Lord, that soon he speed them upwards."

So said he to him; and since we enjoy
  As much in drinking as the thirst is great,
  I could not say how much it did me good.

And the wise Leader: "Now I see the net
  That snares you here, and how ye are set free,
  Why the earth quakes, and wherefore ye rejoice.

Now who thou wast be pleased that I may know;
  And why so many centuries thou hast here
  Been lying, let me gather from thy words."

"In days when the good Titus, with the aid
  Of the supremest King, avenged the wounds
  Whence issued forth the blood by Judas sold,

Under the name that most endures and honors,
  Was I on earth," that spirit made reply,
  "Greatly renowned, but not with faith as yet.

My vocal spirit was so sweet, that Rome
  Me, a Thoulousian, drew unto herself,
  Where I deserved to deck my brows with myrtle.

Statius the people name me still on earth;
  I sang of Thebes, and then of great Achilles;
  But on the way fell with my second burden.

The seeds unto my ardour were the sparks
  Of that celestial flame which heated me,
  Whereby more than a thousand have been fired;

Of the Aeneid speak I, which to me
  A mother was, and was my nurse in song;
  Without this weighed I not a drachma's weight.

And to have lived upon the earth what time
  Virgilius lived, I would accept one sun
  More than I must ere issuing from my ban."

These words towards me made Virgilius turn
  With looks that in their silence said, "Be silent!"
  But yet the power that wills cannot do all things;

For tears and laughter are such pursuivants
  Unto the passion from which each springs forth,
  In the most truthful least the will they follow.

I only smiled, as one who gives the wink;
  Whereat the shade was silent, and it gazed
  Into mine eyes, where most expression dwells;

And, "As thou well mayst consummate a labour
  So great," it said, "why did thy face just now
  Display to me the lightning of a smile?"

Now am I caught on this side and on that;
  One keeps me silent, one to speak conjures me,
  Wherefore I sigh, and I am understood.

"Speak," said my Master, "and be not afraid
  Of speaking, but speak out, and say to him
  What he demands with such solicitude."

Whence I: "Thou peradventure marvellest,
  O antique spirit, at the smile I gave;
  But I will have more wonder seize upon thee.

This one, who guides on high these eyes of mine,
  Is that Virgilius, from whom thou didst learn
  To sing aloud of men and of the Gods.

If other cause thou to my smile imputedst,
  Abandon it as false, and trust it was
  Those words which thou hast spoken concerning him."

Already he was stooping to embrace
  My Teacher's feet; but he said to him: "Brother,
  Do not; for shade thou art, and shade beholdest."

And he uprising: "Now canst thou the sum
  Of love which warms me to thee comprehend,
  When this our vanity I disremember,

Treating a shadow as substantial thing."

Canto XXII

Already was the Angel left behind us,
  The Angel who to the sixth round had turned us,
  Having erased one mark from off my face;

And those who have in justice their desire
  Had said to us, "Beati," in their voices,
  With "sitio," and without more ended it.

And I, more light than through the other passes,
  Went onward so, that without any labour
  I followed upward the swift-footed spirits;

When thus Virgilius began: "The love
  Kindled by virtue aye another kindles,
  Provided outwardly its flame appear.

Hence from the hour that Juvenal descended
  Among us into the infernal Limbo,
  Who made apparent to me thy affection,

My kindliness towards thee was as great
  As ever bound one to an unseen person,
  So that these stairs will now seem short to me.

But tell me, and forgive me as a friend,
  If too great confidence let loose the rein,
  And as a friend now hold discourse with me;

How was it possible within thy breast
  For avarice to find place, 'mid so much wisdom
  As thou wast filled with by thy diligence?"

These words excited Statius at first
  Somewhat to laughter; afterward he answered:
  "Each word of thine is love's dear sign to me.

Verily oftentimes do things appear
  Which give fallacious matter to our doubts,
  Instead of the true causes which are hidden!

Thy question shows me thy belief to be
  That I was niggard in the other life,
  It may be from the circle where I was;

Therefore know thou, that avarice was removed
  Too far from me; and this extravagance
  Thousands of lunar periods have punished.

And were it not that I my thoughts uplifted,
  When I the passage heard where thou exclaimest,
  As if indignant, unto human nature,

'To what impellest thou not, O cursed hunger
  Of gold, the appetite of mortal men?'
  Revolving I should feel the dismal joustings.

Then I perceived the hands could spread too wide
  Their wings in spending, and repented me
  As well of that as of my other sins;

How many with shorn hair shall rise again
  Because of ignorance, which from this sin
  Cuts off repentance living and in death!

And know that the transgression which rebuts
  By direct opposition any sin
  Together with it here its verdure dries.

Therefore if I have been among that folk
  Which mourns its avarice, to purify me,
  For its opposite has this befallen me."

"Now when thou sangest the relentless weapons
  Of the twofold affliction of Jocasta,"
  The singer of the Songs Bucolic said,

"From that which Clio there with thee preludes,
  It does not seem that yet had made thee faithful
  That faith without which no good works suffice.

If this be so, what candles or what sun
  Scattered thy darkness so that thou didst trim
  Thy sails behind the Fisherman thereafter?"

And he to him: "Thou first directedst me
  Towards Parnassus, in its grots to drink,
  And first concerning God didst me enlighten.

Thou didst·as he who walketh in the night,
  Who bears his light behind, which helps him not,
  But wary makes the persons after him,

When thou didst say: 'The age renews itself,
  Justice returns, and man's primeval time,
  And a new progeny descends from heaven.'

Through thee I Poet was, through thee a Christian;
  But that thou better see what I design,
  To color it will I extend my hand.

Already was the world in every part
  Pregnant with the true creed, disseminated
  By messengers of the eternal kingdom;

And thy assertion, spoken of above,
  With the new preachers was in unison;
  Whence I to visit them the custom took.

Then they became so holy in my sight,
  That, when Domitian persecuted them,
  Not without tears of mine were their laments;

And all the while that I on earth remained,
  Them I befriended, and their upright customs
  Made me disparage all the other sects.

And ere I led the Greeks unto the rivers
  Of Thebes, in poetry, I was baptized,
  But out of fear was covertly a Christian,

For a long time professing paganism;
  And this lukewarmness caused me the fourth circle
  To circuit round more than four centuries.

Thou, therefore, who hast raised the covering
  That hid from me whatever good I speak of,
  While in ascending we have time to spare,

Tell me, in what place is our friend Terentius,
  Caecilius, Plautus, Varro, if thou knowest;
  Tell me if they are damned, and in what alley."

"These, Persius and myself, and others many,"
  Replied my Leader, "with that Grecian are
  Whom more than all the rest the Muses suckled,

In the first circle of the prison blind;
  Ofttimes we of the mountain hold discourse
  Which has our nurses ever with itself.

Euripides is with us, Antiphon,
  Simonides, Agatho, and many other
  Greeks who of old their brows with laurel decked.

There some of thine own people may be seen,
  Antigone, Deiphile and Argia,
  And there Ismene mournful as of old.

There she is seen who pointed out Langia;
  There is Tiresias' daughter, and there Thetis,
  And there Deidamia with her sisters."

Silent already were the poets both,
  Attent once more in looking round about,
  From the ascent and from the walls released;

And four handmaidens of the day already
  Were left behind, and at the pole the fifth
  Was pointing upward still its burning horn,

What time my Guide: "I think that tow'rds the edge
  Our dexter shoulders it behoves us turn,
  Circling the mount as we are wont to do."

Thus in that region custom was our ensign;
  And we resumed our way with less suspicion
  For the assenting of that worthy soul

They in advance went on, and I alone
  Behind them, and I listened to their speech,
  Which gave me lessons in the art of song.

But soon their sweet discourses interrupted
  A tree which midway in the road we found,
  With apples sweet and grateful to the smell.

And even as a fir-tree tapers upward
  From bough to bough, so downwardly did that;
  I think in order that no one might climb it.

On that side where our pathway was enclosed
  Fell from the lofty rock a limpid water,
  And spread itself abroad upon the leaves.

The Poets twain unto the tree drew near,
  And from among the foliage a voice
  Cried: "Of this food ye shall have scarcity."

Then said: "More thoughtful Mary was of making
  The marriage feast complete and honorable,
  Than of her mouth which now for you responds;

And for their drink the ancient Roman women
  With water were content; and Daniel
  Disparaged food, and understanding won.

The primal age was beautiful as gold;
  Acorns it made with hunger savorous,
  And nectar every rivulet with thirst.

Honey and locusts were the aliments
  That fed the Baptist in the wilderness;
  Whence he is glorious, and so magnified

As by the Evangel is revealed to you."

Canto XXIII

The while among the verdant leaves mine eyes
  I riveted, as he is wont to do
  Who wastes his life pursuing little birds,

My more than Father said unto me: "Son,
  Come now; because the time that is ordained us
  More usefully should be apportioned out."

I turned my face and no less soon my steps
  Unto the Sages, who were speaking so
  They made the going of no cost to me;

And lo! were heard a song and a lament,
  "Labia mea, Domine," in fashion
  Such that delight and dolence it brought forth.

"O my sweet Father, what is this I hear?"
  Began I; and he answered: "Shades that go
  Perhaps the knot unloosing of their debt."

In the same way that thoughtful pilgrims do,
  Who, unknown people on the road o'ertaking,
  Turn themselves round to them, and do not stop,

Even thus, behind us with a swifter motion
  Coming and passing onward, gazed upon us
  A crowd of spirits silent and devout.

Each in his eyes was dark and cavernous,
  Pallid in face, and so emaciate
  That from the bones the skin did shape itself.

I do not think that so to merest rind
  Could Erisichthon have been withered up
  By famine, when most fear he had of it.

Thinking within myself I said: "Behold,
  This is the folk who lost Jerusalem,
  When Mary made a prey of her own son."

Their sockets were like rings without the gems;
  Whoever in the face of men reads 'omo'
  Might well in these have recognized the 'm.'

Who would believe the odour of an apple,
  Begetting longing, could consume them so,
  And that of water, without knowing how?

I still was wondering what so famished them,
  For the occasion not yet manifest
  Of their emaciation and sad squalor;

And lo! from out the hollow of his head
  His eyes a shade turned on me, and looked keenly;
  Then cried aloud: "What grace to me is this?"

Never should I have known him by his look;
  But in his voice was evident to me
  That which his aspect had suppressed within it.

This spark within me wholly re-enkindled
  My recognition of his altered face,
  And I recalled the features of Forese.

"Ah, do not look at this dry leprosy,"
  Entreated he, "which doth my skin discolor,
  Nor at default of flesh that I may have;

But tell me truth of thee, and who are those
  Two souls, that yonder make for thee an escort;
  Do not delay in speaking unto me."

"That face of thine, which dead I once bewept,
  Gives me for weeping now no lesser grief,"
  I answered him, "beholding it so changed!

But tell me, for God's sake, what thus denudes you?
  Make me not speak while I am marvelling,
  For ill speaks he who's full of other longings."

And he to me: "From the eternal council
  Falls power into the water and the tree
  Behind us left, whereby I grow so thin.

All of this people who lamenting sing,
  For following beyond measure appetite
  In hunger and thirst are here re-sanctified.

Desire to eat and drink enkindles in us
  The scent that issues from the apple-tree,
  And from the spray that sprinkles o'er the verdure;

And not a single time alone, this ground
  Encompassing, is refreshed our pain,—
  I say our pain, and ought to say our solace,—

For the same wish doth lead us to the tree
  Which led the Christ rejoicing to say 'Eli,'
  When with his veins he liberated us."

And I to him: "Forese, from that day
  When for a better life thou changedst worlds,
  Up to this time five years have not rolled round.

If sooner were the power exhausted in thee
  Of sinning more, than thee the hour surprised
  Of that good sorrow which to God reweds us,

How hast thou come up hitherward already?
  I thought to find thee down there underneath,
  Where time for time doth restitution make."

And he to me: "Thus speedily has led me
  To drink of the sweet wormwood of these torments,
  My Nella with her overflowing tears;

She with her prayers devout and with her sighs
  Has drawn me from the coast where one where one awaits,
  And from the other circles set me free.

So much more dear and pleasing is to God
  My little widow, whom so much I loved,
  As in good works she is the more alone;

For the Barbagia of Sardinia
  By far more modest in its women is
  Than the Barbagia I have left her in.

O brother sweet, what wilt thou have me say?
  A future time is in my sight already,
  To which this hour will not be very old,

When from the pulpit shall be interdicted
  To the unblushing womankind of Florence
  To go about displaying breast and paps.

What savages were e'er, what Saracens,
  Who stood in need, to make them covered go,
  Of spiritual or other discipline?

But if the shameless women were assured
  Of what swift Heaven prepares for them, already
  Wide open would they have their mouths to howl;

For if my foresight here deceive me not,
  They shall be sad ere he has bearded cheeks
  Who now is hushed to sleep with lullaby.

O brother, now no longer hide thee from me;
  See that not only I, but all these people
  Are gazing there, where thou dost veil the sun."

Whence I to him: "If thou bring back to mind
  What thou with me hast been and I with thee,
  The present memory will be grievous still.

Out of that life he turned me back who goes
  In front of me, two days agone when round
  The sister of him yonder showed herself,"

And to the sun I pointed. "Through the deep
  Night of the truly dead has this one led me,
  With this true flesh, that follows after him.

Thence his encouragements have led me up,
  Ascending and still circling round the mount
  That you doth straighten, whom the world made crooked.

He says that he will bear me company,
  Till I shall be where Beatrice will be;
  There it behoves me to remain without him.

This is Virgilius, who thus says to me,"
  And him I pointed at; "the other is
  That shade for whom just now shook every slope

Your realm, that from itself discharges him."

Canto XXIV

Nor speech the going, nor the going that
  Slackened; but talking we went bravely on,
  Even as a vessel urged by a good wind.

And shadows, that appeared things doubly dead,
From out the sepulchres of their eyes betrayed
Wonder at me, aware that I was living.

And I, continuing my colloquy,
Said: "Peradventure he goes up more slowly
Than he would do, for other people's sake.

But tell me, if thou knowest, where is Piccarda;
Tell me if any one of note I see
Among this folk that gazes at me so."

"My sister, who, 'twixt beautiful and good,
I know not which was more, triumphs rejoicing
Already in her crown on high Olympus."

So said he first, and then: "'Tis not forbidden
To name each other here, so milked away
Is our resemblance by our dieting.

This," pointing with his finger, "is Buonagiunta,
Buonagiunta, of Lucca; and that face
Beyond him there, more peaked than the others,

Has held the holy Church within his arms;
From Tours was he, and purges by his fasting
Bolsena's eels and the Vernaccia wine."

He named me many others one by one;
And all contented seemed at being named,
So that for this I saw not one dark look.

I saw for hunger bite the empty air
Ubaldin dalla Pila, and Boniface,
Who with his crook had pastured many people.

I saw Messer Marchese, who had leisure
Once at Forli for drinking with less dryness,
And he was one who ne'er felt satisfied.

But as he does who scans, and then doth prize
One more than others, did I him of Lucca,
Who seemed to take most cognizance of me.

He murmured, and I know not what Gentucca
  From that place heard I, where he felt the wound
  Of justice, that doth macerate them so.

"O soul," I said, "that seemest so desirous
  To speak with me, do so that I may hear thee,
  And with thy speech appease thyself and me."

"A maid is born, and wears not yet the veil,"
  Began he, "who to thee shall pleasant make
  My city, howsoever men may blame it.

Thou shalt go on thy way with this prevision;
  If by my murmuring thou hast been deceived,
  True things hereafter will declare it to thee.

But say if him I here behold, who forth
  Evoked the new-invented rhymes, beginning,
  'Ladies, that have intelligence of love?'"

And I to him: "One am I, who, whenever
  Love doth inspire me, note, and in that measure
  Which he within me dictates, singing go."

"O brother, now I see," he said, "the knot
  Which me, the Notary, and Guittone held
  Short of the sweet new style that now I hear.

I do perceive full clearly how your pens
  Go closely following after him who dictates,
  Which with our own forsooth came not to pass;

And he who sets himself to go beyond,
  No difference sees from one style to another;"
  And as if satisfied, he held his peace.

Even as the birds, that winter tow'rds the Nile,
  Sometimes into a phalanx form themselves,
  Then fly in greater haste, and go in file;

In such wise all the people who were there,
  Turning their faces, hurried on their steps,
  Both by their leanness and their wishes light.

And as a man, who weary is with trotting,
  Lets his companions onward go, and walks,
  Until he vents the panting of his chest;

So did Forese let the holy flock
  Pass by, and came with me behind it, saying,
  "When will it be that I again shall see thee?"

"How long," I answered, "I may live, I know not;
  Yet my return will not so speedy be,
  But I shall sooner in desire arrive;

Because the place where I was set to live
  From day to day of good is more depleted,
  And unto dismal ruin seems ordained."

"Now go," he said, "for him most guilty of it
  At a beast's tail behold I dragged along
  Towards the valley where is no repentance.

Faster at every step the beast is going,
  Increasing evermore until it smites him,
  And leaves the body vilely mutilated.

Not long those wheels shall turn," and he uplifted
  His eyes to heaven, "ere shall be clear to thee
  That which my speech no farther can declare.

Now stay behind; because the time so precious
  Is in this kingdom, that I lose too much
  By coming onward thus abreast with thee."

As sometimes issues forth upon a gallop
  A cavalier from out a troop that ride,
  And seeks the honor of the first encounter,

So he with greater strides departed from us;
  And on the road remained I with those two,
  Who were such mighty marshals of the world.

And when before us he had gone so far
  Mine eyes became to him such pursuivants
  As was my understanding to his words,

Appeared to me with laden and living boughs
  Another apple-tree, and not far distant,
  From having but just then turned thitherward.

People I saw beneath it lift their hands,
  And cry I know not what towards the leaves,
  Like little children eager and deluded,

Who pray, and he they pray to doth not answer,
  But, to make very keen their appetite,
  Holds their desire aloft, and hides it not.

Then they departed as if undeceived;
  And now we came unto the mighty tree
  Which prayers and tears so manifold refuses.

"Pass farther onward without drawing near;
  The tree of which Eve ate is higher up,
  And out of that one has this tree been raised."

Thus said I know not who among the branches;
  Whereat Virgilius, Statius, and myself
  Went crowding forward on the side that rises.

"Be mindful," said he, "of the accursed ones
  Formed of the cloud-rack, who inebriate
  Combated Theseus with their double breasts;

And of the Jews who showed them soft in drinking,
  Whence Gideon would not have them for companions
  When he tow'rds Midian the hills descended."

Thus, closely pressed to one of the two borders,
  On passed we, hearing sins of gluttony,
  Followed forsooth by miserable gains;

Then set at large upon the lonely road,
  A thousand steps and more we onward went,
  In contemplation, each without a word.

"What go ye thinking thus, ye three alone?"
  Said suddenly a voice, whereat I started
  As terrified and timid beasts are wont.

I raised my head to see who this might be,
  And never in a furnace was there seen
  Metals or glass so lucent and so red

As one I saw who said: "If it may please you
  To mount aloft, here it behoves you turn;
  This way goes he who goeth after peace."

His aspect had bereft me of my sight,
  So that I turned me back unto my Teachers,
  Like one who goeth as his hearing guides him.

And as, the harbinger of early dawn,
  The air of May doth move and breathe out fragrance,
  Impregnate all with herbage and with flowers,

So did I feel a breeze strike in the midst
  My front, and felt the moving of the plumes
  That breathed around an odour of ambrosia;

And heard it said: "Blessed are they whom grace
  So much illumines, that the love of taste
  Excites not in their breasts too great desire,

Hungering at all times so far as is just."

Canto XXV

Now was it the ascent no hindrance brooked,
  Because the sun had his meridian circle
  To Taurus left, and night to Scorpio;

Wherefore as doth a man who tarries not,
  But goes his way, whate'er to him appear,
  If of necessity the sting transfix him,

In this wise did we enter through the gap,
  Taking the stairway, one before the other,
  Which by its narrowness divides the climbers.

And as the little stork that lifts its wing
  With a desire to fly, and does not venture
  To leave the nest, and lets it downward droop,

Even such was I, with the desire of asking
  Kindled and quenched, unto the motion coming
  He makes who doth address himself to speak.

Not for our pace, though rapid it might be,
  My father sweet forbore, but said: "Let fly
  The bow of speech thou to the barb hast drawn."

With confidence I opened then my mouth,
  And I began: "How can one meagre grow
  There where the need of nutriment applies not?"

"If thou wouldst call to mind how Meleager
  Was wasted by the wasting of a brand,
  This would not," said he, "be to thee so sour;

And wouldst thou think how at each tremulous motion
  Trembles within a mirror your own image;
  That which seems hard would mellow seem to thee.

But that thou mayst content thee in thy wish
  Lo Statius here; and him I call and pray
  He now will be the healer of thy wounds."

"If I unfold to him the eternal vengeance,"
  Responded Statius, "where thou present art,
  Be my excuse that I can naught deny thee."

Then he began: "Son, if these words of mine
  Thy mind doth contemplate and doth receive,
  They'll be thy light unto the How thou sayest.

The perfect blood, which never is drunk up
  Into the thirsty veins, and which remaineth
  Like food that from the table thou removest,

Takes in the heart for all the human members
  Virtue informative, as being that
  Which to be changed to them goes through the veins

Again digest, descends it where 'tis better
  Silent to be than say; and then drops thence
  Upon another's blood in natural vase.

There one together with the other mingles,
  One to be passive meant, the other active
  By reason of the perfect place it springs from;

And being conjoined, begins to operate,
  Coagulating first, then vivifying
  What for its matter it had made consistent.

The active virtue, being made a soul
  As of a plant, (in so far different,
  This on the way is, that arrived already,)

Then works so much, that now it moves and feels
  Like a sea-fungus, and then undertakes
  To organize the powers whose seed it is.

Now, Son, dilates and now distends itself
  The virtue from the generator's heart,
  Where nature is intent on all the members.

But how from animal it man becomes
  Thou dost not see as yet; this is a point
  Which made a wiser man than thou once err

So far, that in his doctrine separate
  He made the soul from possible intellect,
  For he no organ saw by this assumed.

Open thy breast unto the truth that's coming,
  And know that, just as soon as in the foetus
  The articulation of the brain is perfect,

The primal Motor turns to it well pleased
  At so great art of nature, and inspires
  A spirit new with virtue all replete,

Which what it finds there active doth attract
  Into its substance, and becomes one soul,
  Which lives, and feels, and on itself revolves.

And that thou less may wonder at my word,
  Behold the sun's heat, which becometh wine,
  Joined to the juice that from the vine distils.

Whenever Lachesis has no more thread,
  It separates from the flesh, and virtually
  Bears with itself the human and divine;

The other faculties are voiceless all;
  The memory, the intelligence, and the will
  In action far more vigorous than before.

Without a pause it falleth of itself
  In marvellous way on one shore or the other;
  There of its roads it first is cognizant.

Soon as the place there circumscribeth it,
  The virtue informative rays round about,
  As, and as much as, in the living members.

And even as the air, when full of rain,
  By alien rays that are therein reflected,
  With divers colors shows itself adorned,

So there the neighboring air doth shape itself
  Into that form which doth impress upon it
  Virtually the soul that has stood still.

And then in manner of the little flame,
  Which followeth the fire where'er it shifts,
  After the spirit followeth its new form.

Since afterwards it takes from this its semblance,
  It is called shade; and thence it organizes
  Thereafter every sense, even to the sight.

Thence is it that we speak, and thence we laugh;
  Thence is it that we form the tears and sighs,
  That on the mountain thou mayhap hast heard.

According as impress us our desires
  And other affections, so the shade is shaped,
  And this is cause of what thou wonderest at."

And now unto the last of all the circles
  Had we arrived, and to the right hand turned,
  And were attentive to another care.

There the embankment shoots forth flames of fire,
  And upward doth the cornice breathe a blast
  That drives them back, and from itself sequesters.

Hence we must needs go on the open side,
  And one by one; and I did fear the fire
  On this side, and on that the falling down.

My Leader said: "Along this place one ought
  To keep upon the eyes a tightened rein,
  Seeing that one so easily might err."

"Summae Deus clementiae," in the bosom
  Of the great burning chanted then I heard,
  Which made me no less eager to turn round;

And spirits saw I walking through the flame;
  Wherefore I looked, to my own steps and theirs
  Apportioning my sight from time to time.

After the close which to that hymn is made,
  Aloud they shouted, "Virum non cognosco;"
  Then recommenced the hymn with voices low.

This also ended, cried they: "To the wood
  Diana ran, and drove forth Helice
  Therefrom, who had of Venus felt the poison."

Then to their song returned they; then the wives
  They shouted, and the husbands who were chaste.
  As virtue and the marriage vow imposes.

And I believe that them this mode suffices,
  For all the time the fire is burning them;
  With such care is it needful, and such food,

That the last wound of all should be closed up.

Canto XXVI

While on the brink thus one before the other
  We went upon our way, oft the good Master
  Said: "Take thou heed! suffice it that I warn thee."

On the right shoulder smote me now the sun,
  That, raying out, already the whole west
  Changed from its azure aspect into white.

And with my shadow did I make the flame
  Appear more red; and even to such a sign
  Shades saw I many, as they went, give heed.

This was the cause that gave them a beginning
  To speak of me; and to themselves began they
  To say: "That seems not a factitious body!"

Then towards me, as far as they could come,
  Came certain of them, always with regard
  Not to step forth where they would not be burned.

"O thou who goest, not from being slower
  But reverent perhaps, behind the others,
  Answer me, who in thirst and fire am burning.

Nor to me only is thine answer needful;
  For all of these have greater thirst for it
  Than for cold water Ethiop or Indian.

Tell us how is it that thou makest thyself
  A wall unto the sun, as if thou hadst not
  Entered as yet into the net of death."

Thus one of them addressed me, and I straight
  Should have revealed myself, were I not bent
  On other novelty that then appeared.

For through the middle of the burning road
  There came a people face to face with these,
  Which held me in suspense with gazing at them.

There see I hastening upon either side
  Each of the shades, and kissing one another
  Without a pause, content with brief salute.

Thus in the middle of their brown battalions
  Muzzle to muzzle one ant meets another
  Perchance to spy their journey or their fortune.

No sooner is the friendly greeting ended,
  Or ever the first footstep passes onward,
  Each one endeavours to outcry the other;

The new-come people: "Sodom and Gomorrah!"
  The rest: "Into the cow Pasiphae enters,
  So that the bull unto her lust may run!"

Then as the cranes, that to Riphaean mountains
  Might fly in part, and part towards the sands,
  These of the frost, those of the sun avoidant,

One folk is going, and the other coming,
  And weeping they return to their first songs,
  And to the cry that most befitteth them;

And close to me approached, even as before,
  The very same who had entreated me,
  Attent to listen in their countenance.

I, who their inclination twice had seen,
  Began: "O souls secure in the possession,
  Whene'er it may be, of a state of peace,

Neither unripe nor ripened have remained
  My members upon earth, but here are with me
  With their own blood and their articulations.

I go up here to be no longer blind;
  A Lady is above, who wins this grace,
  Whereby the mortal through your world I bring.

But as your greatest longing satisfied
  May soon become, so that the Heaven may house you
  Which full of love is, and most amply spreads,

Tell me, that I again in books may write it,
  Who are you, and what is that multitude
  Which goes upon its way behind your backs?"

Not otherwise with wonder is bewildered
  The mountaineer, and staring round is dumb,
  When rough and rustic to the town he goes,

Than every shade became in its appearance;
  But when they of their stupor were disburdened,
  Which in high hearts is quickly quieted,

"Blessed be thou, who of our border-lands,"
  He recommenced who first had questioned us,
  "Experience freightest for a better life.

The folk that comes not with us have offended
  In that for which once Caesar, triumphing,
  Heard himself called in contumely, 'Queen.'

Therefore they separate, exclaiming, 'Sodom!'
  Themselves reproving, even as thou hast heard,
  And add unto their burning by their shame.

Our own transgression was hermaphrodite;
  But because we observed not human law,
  Following like unto beasts our appetite,

In our opprobrium by us is read,
  When we part company, the name of her
  Who bestialized herself in bestial wood.

Now knowest thou our acts, and what our crime was;
  Wouldst thou perchance by name know who we are,
  There is not time to tell, nor could I do it.

Thy wish to know me shall in sooth be granted;
  I'm Guido Guinicelli, and now purge me,
  Having repented ere the hour extreme."

The same that in the sadness of Lycurgus
  Two sons became, their mother re-beholding,
  Such I became, but rise not to such height,

The moment I heard name himself the father
  Of me and of my betters, who had ever
  Practised the sweet and gracious rhymes of love;

And without speech and hearing thoughtfully
  For a long time I went, beholding him,
  Nor for the fire did I approach him nearer.

When I was fed with looking, utterly
  Myself I offered ready for his service,
  With affirmation that compels belief.

And he to me: "Thou leavest footprints such
  In me, from what I hear, and so distinct,
  Lethe cannot efface them, nor make dim.

But if thy words just now the truth have sworn,
  Tell me what is the cause why thou displayest
  In word and look that dear thou holdest me?"

And I to him: "Those dulcet lays of yours
  Which, long as shall endure our modern fashion,
  Shall make for ever dear their very ink!"

"O brother," said he, "he whom I point out,"
  And here he pointed at a spirit in front,
  "Was of the mother tongue a better smith.

Verses of love and proses of romance,
  He mastered all; and let the idiots talk,
  Who think the Lemosin surpasses him.

To clamour more than truth they turn their faces,
  And in this way establish their opinion,
  Ere art or reason has by them been heard.

Thus many ancients with Guittone did,
  From cry to cry still giving him applause,
  Until the truth has conquered with most persons.

Now, if thou hast such ample privilege
  'Tis granted thee to go unto the cloister
  Wherein is Christ the abbot of the college,

To him repeat for me a Paternoster,
  So far as needful to us of this world,
  Where power of sinning is no longer ours."

Then, to give place perchance to one behind,
  Whom he had near, he vanished in the fire
  As fish in water going to the bottom.

I moved a little tow'rds him pointed out,
  And said that to his name my own desire
  An honorable place was making ready.

He of his own free will began to say:
  'Tan m' abellis vostre cortes deman,
  Que jeu nom' puesc ni vueill a vos cobrire;

Jeu sui Arnaut, que plor e vai chantan;
  Consiros vei la passada folor,
  E vei jauzen lo jorn qu' esper denan.

Ara vus prec per aquella valor,
  Que vus condus al som de la scalina,
  Sovenga vus a temprar ma dolor.'*

Then hid him in the fire that purifies them.

* So pleases me your courteous demand,
  I cannot and I will not hide me from you.
I am Arnaut, who weep and singing go;
  Contrite I see the folly of the past,
  And joyous see the hoped-for day before me.
Therefore do I implore you, by that power
  Which guides you to the summit of the stairs,
  Be mindful to assuage my suffering!

Canto XXVII

As when he vibrates forth his earliest rays,
  In regions where his Maker shed his blood,
  (The Ebro falling under lofty Libra,

And waters in the Ganges burnt with noon,)
  So stood the Sun; hence was the day departing,
  When the glad Angel of God appeared to us.

Outside the flame he stood upon the verge,
  And chanted forth, "Beati mundo corde,"
  In voice by far more living than our own.

Then: "No one farther goes, souls sanctified,
  If first the fire bite not; within it enter,
  And be not deaf unto the song beyond."

When we were close beside him thus he said;
  Wherefore e'en such became I, when I heard him,
  As he is who is put into the grave.

Upon my clasped hands I straightened me,
  Scanning the fire, and vividly recalling
  The human bodies I had once seen burned.

Towards me turned themselves my good Conductors,
  And unto me Virgilius said: "My son,
  Here may indeed be torment, but not death.

Remember thee, remember! and if I
  On Geryon have safely guided thee,
  What shall I do now I am nearer God?

Believe for certain, shouldst thou stand a full
  Millennium in the bosom of this flame,
  It could not make thee bald a single hair.

And if perchance thou think that I deceive thee,
  Draw near to it, and put it to the proof
  With thine own hands upon thy garment's hem.

Now lay aside, now lay aside all fear,
  Turn hitherward, and onward come securely;"
  And I still motionless, and 'gainst my conscience!

Seeing me stand still motionless and stubborn,
  Somewhat disturbed he said: "Now look thou, Son,
  'Twixt Beatrice and thee there is this wall."

As at the name of Thisbe oped his lids
  The dying Pyramus, and gazed upon her,
  What time the mulberry became vermilion,

Even thus, my obduracy being softened,
  I turned to my wise Guide, hearing the name
  That in my memory evermore is welling.

Whereat he wagged his head, and said: "How now?
  Shall we stay on this side?" then smiled as one
  Does at a child who's vanquished by an apple.

Then into the fire in front of me he entered,
  Beseeching Statius to come after me,
  Who a long way before divided us.

When I was in it, into molten glass
  I would have cast me to refresh myself,
  So without measure was the burning there!

And my sweet Father, to encourage me,
  Discoursing still of Beatrice went on,
  Saying: "Her eyes I seem to see already!"

A voice, that on the other side was singing,
  Directed us, and we, attent alone
  On that, came forth where the ascent began.

"Venite, benedicti Patris mei,"
  Sounded within a splendor, which was there
  Such it o'ercame me, and I could not look.

"The sun departs," it added, "and night cometh;
  Tarry ye not, but onward urge your steps,
  So long as yet the west becomes not dark."

Straight forward through the rock the path ascended
  In such a way that I cut off the rays
  Before me of the sun, that now was low.

And of few stairs we yet had made assay,
  Ere by the vanished shadow the sun's setting
  Behind us we perceived, I and my Sages.

And ere in all its parts immeasurable
  The horizon of one aspect had become,
  And Night her boundless dispensation held,

Each of us of a stair had made his bed;
  Because the nature of the mount took from us
  The power of climbing, more than the delight.

Even as in ruminating passive grow
  The goats, who have been swift and venturesome
  Upon the mountain-tops ere they were fed,

Hushed in the shadow, while the sun is hot,
  Watched by the herdsman, who upon his staff
  Is leaning, and in leaning tendeth them;

And as the shepherd, lodging out of doors,
  Passes the night beside his quiet flock,
  Watching that no wild beast may scatter it,

Such at that hour were we, all three of us,
  I like the goat, and like the herdsmen they,
  Begirt on this side and on that by rocks.

Little could there be seen of things without;
  But through that little I beheld the stars
  More luminous and larger than their wont.

Thus ruminating, and beholding these,
  Sleep seized upon me,—sleep, that oftentimes
  Before a deed is done has tidings of it.

It was the hour, I think, when from the East
  First on the mountain Citherea beamed,
  Who with the fire of love seems always burning;

Youthful and beautiful in dreams methought
  I saw a lady walking in a meadow,
  Gathering flowers; and singing she was saying:

"Know whosoever may my name demand
  That I am Leah, and go moving round
  My beauteous hands to make myself a garland.

To please me at the mirror, here I deck me,
  But never does my sister Rachel leave
  Her looking-glass, and sitteth all day long.

To see her beauteous eyes as eager is she,
  As I am to adorn me with my hands;
  Her, seeing, and me, doing satisfies."

And now before the antelucan splendors
  That unto pilgrims the more grateful rise,
  As, home-returning, less remote they lodge,

The darkness fled away on every side,
  And slumber with it; whereupon I rose,
  Seeing already the great Masters risen.

"That apple sweet, which through so many branches
  The care of mortals goeth in pursuit of,
  To-day shall put in peace thy hungerings."

Speaking to me, Virgilius of such words
  As these made use; and never were there guerdons
  That could in pleasantness compare with these.

Such longing upon longing came upon me
  To be above, that at each step thereafter
  For flight I felt in me the pinions growing.

When underneath us was the stairway all
  Run o'er, and we were on the highest step,
  Virgilius fastened upon me his eyes,

And said: "The temporal fire and the eternal,
  Son, thou hast seen, and to a place art come
  Where of myself no farther I discern.

By intellect and art I here have brought thee;
  Take thine own pleasure for thy guide henceforth;
  Beyond the steep ways and the narrow art thou.

Behold the sun, that shines upon thy forehead;
  Behold the grass, the flowerets, and the shrubs
  Which of itself alone this land produces.

Until rejoicing come the beauteous eyes
  Which weeping caused me to come unto thee,
  Thou canst sit down, and thou canst walk among them.

Expect no more or word or sign from me;
  Free and upright and sound is thy free-will,
  And error were it not to do its bidding;

Thee o'er thyself I therefore crown and mitre!"

Canto XXVIII

Eager already to search in and round
  The heavenly forest, dense and living-green,
  Which tempered to the eyes the new-born day,

Withouten more delay I left the bank,
  Taking the level country slowly, slowly
  Over the soil that everywhere breathes fragrance.

A softly-breathing air, that no mutation
  Had in itself, upon the forehead smote me
  No heavier blow than of a gentle wind,

Whereat the branches, lightly tremulous,
  Did all of them bow downward toward that side
  Where its first shadow casts the Holy Mountain;

Yet not from their upright direction swayed,
  So that the little birds upon their tops
  Should leave the practice of each art of theirs;

But with full ravishment the hours of prime,
  Singing, received they in the midst of leaves,
  That ever bore a burden to their rhymes,

Such as from branch to branch goes gathering on
  Through the pine forest on the shore of Chiassi,
  When Eolus unlooses the Sirocco.

Already my slow steps had carried me
  Into the ancient wood so far, that I
  Could not perceive where I had entered it.

And lo! my further course a stream cut off,
  Which tow'rd the left hand with its little waves
  Bent down the grass that on its margin sprang.

All waters that on earth most limpid are
  Would seem to have within themselves some mixture
  Compared with that which nothing doth conceal,

Although it moves on with a brown, brown current
  Under the shade perpetual, that never
  Ray of the sun lets in, nor of the moon.

With feet I stayed, and with mine eyes I passed
  Beyond the rivulet, to look upon
  The great variety of the fresh may.

And there appeared to me (even as appears
  Suddenly something that doth turn aside
  Through very wonder every other thought)

A lady all alone, who went along
  Singing and culling floweret after floweret,
  With which her pathway was all painted over.

"Ah, beauteous lady, who in rays of love
  Dost warm thyself, if I may trust to looks,
  Which the heart's witnesses are wont to be,

May the desire come unto thee to draw
  Near to this river's bank," I said to her,
  "So much that I might hear what thou art singing.

Thou makest me remember where and what
  Proserpina that moment was when lost
  Her mother her, and she herself the Spring."

As turns herself, with feet together pressed
  And to the ground, a lady who is dancing,
  And hardly puts one foot before the other,

On the vermilion and the yellow flowerets
  She turned towards me, not in other wise
  Than maiden who her modest eyes casts down;

And my entreaties made to be content,
  So near approaching, that the dulcet sound
  Came unto me together with its meaning

As soon as she was where the grasses are.
  Bathed by the waters of the beauteous river,
  To lift her eyes she granted me the boon.

I do not think there shone so great a light
  Under the lids of Venus, when transfixed
  By her own son, beyond his usual custom!

Erect upon the other bank she smiled,
  Bearing full many colors in her hands,
  Which that high land produces without seed.

Apart three paces did the river make us;
  But Hellespont, where Xerxes passed across,
  (A curb still to all human arrogance,)

More hatred from Leander did not suffer
  For rolling between Sestos and Abydos,
  Than that from me, because it oped not then.

"Ye are new-comers; and because I smile,"
  Began she, "peradventure, in this place
  Elect to human nature for its nest,

Some apprehension keeps you marvelling;
  But the psalm 'Delectasti' giveth light
  Which has the power to uncloud your intellect.

And thou who foremost art, and didst entreat me,
  Speak, if thou wouldst hear more; for I came ready
  To all thy questionings, as far as needful."

"The water," said I, "and the forest's sound,
  Are combating within me my new faith
  In something which I heard opposed to this."

Whence she: "I will relate how from its cause
  Proceedeth that which maketh thee to wonder,
  And purge away the cloud that smites upon thee.

The Good Supreme, sole in itself delighting,
  Created man good, and this goodly place
  Gave him as hansel of eternal peace.

By his default short while he sojourned here;
  By his default to weeping and to toil
  He changed his innocent laughter and sweet play.

That the disturbance which below is made
  By exhalations of the land and water,
  (Which far as may be follow after heat,)

Might not upon mankind wage any war,
  This mount ascended tow'rds the heaven so high,
  And is exempt, from there where it is locked.

Now since the universal atmosphere
  Turns in a circuit with the primal motion
  Unless the circle is broken on some side,

Upon this height, that all is disengaged
  In living ether, doth this motion strike
  And make the forest sound, for it is dense;

And so much power the stricken plant possesses
  That with its virtue it impregns the air,
  And this, revolving, scatters it around;

And yonder earth, according as 'tis worthy
  In self or in its clime, conceives and bears
  Of divers qualities the divers trees;

It should not seem a marvel then on earth,
  This being heard, whenever any plant
  Without seed manifest there taketh root.

And thou must know, this holy table-land
  In which thou art is full of every seed,
  And fruit has in it never gathered there.

The water which thou seest springs not from vein
  Restored by vapour that the cold condenses,
  Like to a stream that gains or loses breath;

But issues from a fountain safe and certain,
  Which by the will of God as much regains
  As it discharges, open on two sides.

Upon this side with virtue it descends,
  Which takes away all memory of sin;
  On that, of every good deed done restores it.

Here Lethe, as upon the other side
  Eunoe, it is called; and worketh not
  If first on either side it be not tasted.

This every other savour doth transcend;
  And notwithstanding slaked so far may be
  Thy thirst, that I reveal to thee no more,

I'll give thee a corollary still in grace,
  Nor think my speech will be to thee less dear
  If it spread out beyond my promise to thee.

Those who in ancient times have feigned in song
  The Age of Gold and its felicity,
  Dreamed of this place perhaps upon Parnassus.

Here was the human race in innocence;
  Here evermore was Spring, and every fruit;
  This is the nectar of which each one speaks."

Then backward did I turn me wholly round
  Unto my Poets, and saw that with a smile
  They had been listening to these closing words;

Then to the beautiful lady turned mine eyes.

Canto XXIX

Singing like unto an enamoured lady
  She, with the ending of her words, continued:
  "Beati quorum tecta sunt peccata."

And even as Nymphs, that wandered all alone
  Among the sylvan shadows, sedulous
  One to avoid and one to see the sun,

She then against the stream moved onward, going
  Along the bank, and I abreast of her,
  Her little steps with little steps attending.

Between her steps and mine were not a hundred,
  When equally the margins gave a turn,
  In such a way, that to the East I faced.

Nor even thus our way continued far
  Before the lady wholly turned herself
  Unto me, saying, "Brother, look and listen!"

And lo! a sudden lustre ran across
  On every side athwart the spacious forest,
  Such that it made me doubt if it were lightning.

But since the lightning ceases as it comes,
  And that continuing brightened more and more,
  Within my thought I said, "What thing is this?"

And a delicious melody there ran
  Along the luminous air, whence holy zeal
  Made me rebuke the hardihood of Eve;

For there where earth and heaven obedient were,
  The woman only, and but just created,
  Could not endure to stay 'neath any veil;

Underneath which had she devoutly stayed,
  I sooner should have tasted those delights
  Ineffable, and for a longer time.

While 'mid such manifold first-fruits I walked
  Of the eternal pleasure all enrapt,
  And still solicitous of more delights,

In front of us like an enkindled fire
  Became the air beneath the verdant boughs,
  And the sweet sound as singing now was heard.

O Virgins sacrosanct! if ever hunger,
  Vigils, or cold for you I have endured,
  The occasion spurs me their reward to claim!

Now Helicon must needs pour forth for me,
  And with her choir Urania must assist me,
  To put in verse things difficult to think.

A little farther on, seven trees of gold
  In semblance the long space still intervening
  Between ourselves and them did counterfeit;

But when I had approached so near to them
  The common object, which the sense deceives,
  Lost not by distance any of its marks,

The faculty that lends discourse to reason
  Did apprehend that they were candlesticks,
  And in the voices of the song "Hosanna!"

Above them flamed the harness beautiful,
  Far brighter than the moon in the serene
  Of midnight, at the middle of her month.

I turned me round, with admiration filled,
  To good Virgilius, and he answered me
  With visage no less full of wonderment.

Then back I turned my face to those high things,
  Which moved themselves towards us so sedately,
  They had been distanced by new-wedded brides.

The lady chid me: "Why dost thou burn only
  So with affection for the living lights,
  And dost not look at what comes after them?"

Then saw I people, as behind their leaders,
  Coming behind them, garmented in white,
  And such a whiteness never was on earth.

The water on my left flank was resplendent,
  And back to me reflected my left side,
  E'en as a mirror, if I looked therein.

When I upon my margin had such post
  That nothing but the stream divided us,
  Better to see I gave my steps repose;

And I beheld the flamelets onward go,
  Leaving behind themselves the air depicted,
  And they of trailing pennons had the semblance,

So that it overhead remained distinct
  With sevenfold lists, all of them of the colors
  Whence the sun's bow is made, and Delia's girdle.

These standards to the rearward longer were
  Than was my sight; and, as it seemed to me,
  Ten paces were the outermost apart.

Under so fair a heaven as I describe
  The four and twenty Elders, two by two,
  Came on incoronate with flower-de-luce.

They all of them were singing: "Blessed thou
  Among the daughters of Adam art, and blessed
  For evermore shall be thy loveliness."

After the flowers and other tender grasses
  In front of me upon the other margin
  Were disencumbered of that race elect,

Even as in heaven star followeth after star,
  There came close after them four animals,
  Incoronate each one with verdant leaf.

Plumed with six wings was every one of them,
  The plumage full of eyes; the eyes of Argus
  If they were living would be such as these.

Reader! to trace their forms no more I waste
  My rhymes; for other spendings press me so,
  That I in this cannot be prodigal.

But read Ezekiel, who depicteth them
  As he beheld them from the region cold
  Coming with cloud, with whirlwind, and with fire;

And such as thou shalt find them in his pages,
  Such were they here; saving that in their plumage
  John is with me, and differeth from him.

The interval between these four contained
  A chariot triumphal on two wheels,
  Which by a Griffin's neck came drawn along;

And upward he extended both his wings
  Between the middle list and three and three,
  So that he injured none by cleaving it.

So high they rose that they were lost to sight;
  His limbs were gold, so far as he was bird,
  And white the others with vermilion mingled.

Not only Rome with no such splendid car
  E'er gladdened Africanus, or Augustus,
  But poor to it that of the Sun would be,—

That of the Sun, which swerving was burnt up
  At the importunate orison of Earth,
  When Jove was so mysteriously just.

Three maidens at the right wheel in a circle
  Came onward dancing; one so very red
  That in the fire she hardly had been noted.

The second was as if her flesh and bones
  Had all been fashioned out of emerald;
  The third appeared as snow but newly fallen.

And now they seemed conducted by the white,
  Now by the red, and from the song of her
  The others took their step, or slow or swift.

Upon the left hand four made holiday
  Vested in purple, following the measure
  Of one of them with three eyes m her head.

In rear of all the group here treated of
  Two old men I beheld, unlike in habit,
  But like in gait, each dignified and grave.

One showed himself as one of the disciples
  Of that supreme Hippocrates, whom nature
  Made for the animals she holds most dear;

Contrary care the other manifested,
  With sword so shining and so sharp, it caused
  Terror to me on this side of the river.

Thereafter four I saw of humble aspect,
  And behind all an aged man alone
  Walking in sleep with countenance acute.

And like the foremost company these seven
  Were habited; yet of the flower-de-luce
  No garland round about the head they wore,

But of the rose, and other flowers vermilion;
  At little distance would the sight have sworn
  That all were in a flame above their brows.

And when the car was opposite to me
  Thunder was heard; and all that folk august
  Seemed to have further progress interdicted,

There with the vanward ensigns standing still.

Canto XXX

When the Septentrion of the highest heaven
  (Which never either setting knew or rising,
  Nor veil of other cloud than that of sin,

And which made every one therein aware
  Of his own duty, as the lower makes
  Whoever turns the helm to come to port)

Motionless halted, the veracious people,
  That came at first between it and the Griffin,
  Turned themselves to the car, as to their peace.

And one of them, as if by Heaven commissioned,
  Singing, "Veni, sponsa, de Libano"
  Shouted three times, and all the others after.

Even as the Blessed at the final summons
  Shall rise up quickened each one from his cavern,
  Uplifting light the reinvested flesh,

So upon that celestial chariot
  A hundred rose 'ad vocem tanti senis,'
  Ministers and messengers of life eternal.

They all were saying, "Benedictus qui venis,"
  And, scattering flowers above and round about,
  "Manibus o date lilia plenis."

Ere now have I beheld, as day began,
  The eastern hemisphere all tinged with rose,
  And the other heaven with fair serene adorned;

And the sun's face, uprising, overshadowed
  So that by tempering influence of vapours
  For a long interval the eye sustained it;

Thus in the bosom of a cloud of flowers
  Which from those hands angelical ascended,
  And downward fell again inside and out,

Over her snow-white veil with olive cinct
  Appeared a lady under a green mantle,
  Vested in color of the living flame.

And my own spirit, that already now
  So long a time had been, that in her presence
  Trembling with awe it had not stood abashed,

Without more knowledge having by mine eyes,
  Through occult virtue that from her proceeded
  Of ancient love the mighty influence felt.

As soon as on my vision smote the power
  Sublime, that had already pierced me through
  Ere from my boyhood I had yet come forth,

To the left hand I turned with that reliance
  With which the little child runs to his mother,
  When he has fear, or when he is afflicted,

To say unto Virgilius: "Not a drachm
  Of blood remains in me, that does not tremble;
  I know the traces of the ancient flame."

But us Virgilius of himself deprived
  Had left, Virgilius, sweetest of all fathers,
  Virgilius, to whom I for safety gave me:

Nor whatsoever lost the ancient mother
  Availed my cheeks now purified from dew,
  That weeping they should not again be darkened.

"Dante, because Virgilius has departed
  Do not weep yet, do not weep yet awhile;
  For by another sword thou need'st must weep."

E'en as an admiral, who on poop and prow
  Comes to behold the people that are working
  In other ships, and cheers them to well-doing,

Upon the left hand border of the car,
  When at the sound I turned of my own name,
  Which of necessity is here recorded,

I saw the Lady, who erewhile appeared
  Veiled underneath the angelic festival,
  Direct her eyes to me across the river.

Although the veil, that from her head descended,
  Encircled with the foliage of Minerva,
  Did not permit her to appear distinctly,

In attitude still royally majestic
  Continued she, like unto one who speaks,
  And keeps his warmest utterance in reserve:

"Look at me well; in sooth I'm Beatrice!
  How didst thou deign to come unto the Mountain?
  Didst thou not know that man is happy here?"

Mine eyes fell downward into the clear fountain,
  But, seeing myself therein, I sought the grass,
  So great a shame did weigh my forehead down.

As to the son the mother seems superb,
  So she appeared to me; for somewhat bitter
  Tasteth the savour of severe compassion.

Silent became she, and the Angels sang
  Suddenly, "In te, Domine, speravi:"
  But beyond 'pedes meos' did not pass.

Even as the snow among the living rafters
  Upon the back of Italy congeals,
  Blown on and drifted by Sclavonian winds,

And then, dissolving, trickles through itself
  Whene'er the land that loses shadow breathes,
  So that it seems a fire that melts a taper;

E'en thus was I without a tear or sigh,
  Before the song of those who sing for ever
  After the music of the eternal spheres.

But when I heard in their sweet melodies
  Compassion for me, more than had they said,
  "O wherefore, lady, dost thou thus upbraid him?"

The ice, that was about my heart congealed,
  To air and water changed, and in my anguish
  Through mouth and eyes came gushing from my breast.

She, on the right-hand border of the car
  Still firmly standing, to those holy beings
  Thus her discourse directed afterwards:

"Ye keep your watch in the eternal day,
  So that nor night nor sleep can steal from you
  One step the ages make upon their path;

Therefore my answer is with greater care,
  That he may hear me who is weeping yonder,
  So that the sin and dole be of one measure.

Not only by the work of those great wheels,
  That destine every seed unto some end,
  According as the stars are in conjunction,

But by the largess of celestial graces,
  Which have such lofty vapours for their rain
  That near to them our sight approaches not,

Such had this man become in his new life
  Potentially, that every righteous habit
  Would have made admirable proof in him;

But so much more malignant and more savage
  Becomes the land untilled and with bad seed,
  The more good earthly vigour it possesses.

Some time did I sustain him with my look;
  Revealing unto him my youthful eyes,
  I led him with me turned in the right way.

As soon as ever of my second age
  I was upon the threshold and changed life,
  Himself from me he took and gave to others.

When from the flesh to spirit I ascended,
  And beauty and virtue were in me increased,
  I was to him less dear and less delightful;

And into ways untrue he turned his steps,
  Pursuing the false images of good,
  That never any promises fulfil;

Nor prayer for inspiration me availed,
  By means of which in dreams and otherwise
  I called him back, so little did he heed them.

So low he fell, that all appliances
  For his salvation were already short,
  Save showing him the people of perdition.

For this I visited the gates of death,
  And unto him, who so far up has led him,
  My intercessions were with weeping borne.

God's lofty fiat would be violated,
  If Lethe should be passed, and if such viands
  Should tasted be, withouten any scot

Of penitence, that gushes forth in tears."

Canto XXXI

"O thou who art beyond the sacred river,"
  Turning to me the point of her discourse,
  That edgewise even had seemed to me so keen,

She recommenced, continuing without pause,
  "Say, say if this be true; to such a charge,
  Thy own confession needs must be conjoined."

My faculties were in so great confusion,
  That the voice moved, but sooner was extinct
  Than by its organs it was set at large.

Awhile she waited; then she said: "What thinkest?
  Answer me; for the mournful memories
  In thee not yet are by the waters injured."

Confusion and dismay together mingled
  Forced such a Yes! from out my mouth, that sight
  Was needful to the understanding of it.

Even as a cross-bow breaks, when 'tis discharged
  Too tensely drawn the bowstring and the bow,
  And with less force the arrow hits the mark,

So I gave way beneath that heavy burden,
  Outpouring in a torrent tears and sighs,
  And the voice flagged upon its passage forth.

Whence she to me: "In those desires of mine
  Which led thee to the loving of that good,
  Beyond which there is nothing to aspire to,

What trenches lying traverse or what chains
  Didst thou discover, that of passing onward
  Thou shouldst have thus despoiled thee of the hope?

And what allurements or what vantages
  Upon the forehead of the others showed,
  That thou shouldst turn thy footsteps unto them?"

After the heaving of a bitter sigh,
  Hardly had I the voice to make response,
  And with fatigue my lips did fashion it.

Weeping I said: "The things that present were
  With their false pleasure turned aside my steps,
  Soon as your countenance concealed itself."

And she: "Shouldst thou be silent, or deny
  What thou confessest, not less manifest
  Would be thy fault, by such a Judge 'tis known.

But when from one's own cheeks comes bursting forth
  The accusal of the sin, in our tribunal
  Against the edge the wheel doth turn itself.

But still, that thou mayst feel a greater shame
  For thy transgression, and another time
  Hearing the Sirens thou mayst be more strong,

Cast down the seed of weeping and attend;
  So shalt thou hear, how in an opposite way
  My buried flesh should have directed thee.

Never to thee presented art or nature
  Pleasure so great as the fair limbs wherein
  I was enclosed, which scattered are in earth.

And if the highest pleasure thus did fail thee
  By reason of my death, what mortal thing
  Should then have drawn thee into its desire?

Thou oughtest verily at the first shaft
  Of things fallacious to have risen up
  To follow me, who was no longer such.

Thou oughtest not to have stooped thy pinions downward
  To wait for further blows, or little girl,
  Or other vanity of such brief use.

The callow birdlet waits for two or three,
  But to the eyes of those already fledged,
  In vain the net is spread or shaft is shot."

Even as children silent in their shame
  Stand listening with their eyes upon the ground,
  And conscious of their fault, and penitent;

So was I standing; and she said: "If thou
  In hearing sufferest pain, lift up thy beard
  And thou shalt feel a greater pain in seeing."

With less resistance is a robust holm
  Uprooted, either by a native wind
  Or else by that from regions of Iarbas,

Than I upraised at her command my chin;
  And when she by the beard the face demanded,
  Well I perceived the venom of her meaning.

And as my countenance was lifted up,
  Mine eye perceived those creatures beautiful
  Had rested from the strewing of the flowers;

And, still but little reassured, mine eyes
  Saw Beatrice turned round towards the monster,
  That is one person only in two natures.

Beneath her veil, beyond the margent green,
  She seemed to me far more her ancient self
  To excel, than others here, when she was here.

So pricked me then the thorn of penitence,
  That of all other things the one which turned me
  Most to its love became the most my foe.

Such self-conviction stung me at the heart
  O'erpowered I fell, and what I then became
  She knoweth who had furnished me the cause.

Then, when the heart restored my outward sense,
  The lady I had found alone, above me
  I saw, and she was saying, "Hold me, hold me."

Up to my throat she in the stream had drawn me,
  And, dragging me behind her, she was moving
  Upon the water lightly as a shuttle.

When I was near unto the blessed shore,
  "Asperges me," I heard so sweetly sung,
  Remember it I cannot, much less write it.

The beautiful lady opened wide her arms,
  Embraced my head, and plunged me underneath,
  Where I was forced to swallow of the water.

Then forth she drew me, and all dripping brought
  Into the dance of the four beautiful,
  And each one with her arm did cover me.

'We here are Nymphs, and in the Heaven are stars;
  Ere Beatrice descended to the world,
  We as her handmaids were appointed her.

We'll lead thee to her eyes; but for the pleasant
  Light that within them is, shall sharpen thine
  The three beyond, who more profoundly look.'

Thus singing they began; and afterwards
  Unto the Griffin's breast they led me with them,
  Where Beatrice was standing, turned towards us.

"See that thou dost not spare thine eyes," they said;
  "Before the emeralds have we stationed thee,
  Whence Love aforetime drew for thee his weapons."

A thousand longings, hotter than the flame,
  Fastened mine eyes upon those eyes relucent,
  That still upon the Griffin steadfast stayed.

As in a glass the sun, not otherwise
  Within them was the twofold monster shining,
  Now with the one, now with the other nature.

Think, Reader, if within myself I marvelled,
  When I beheld the thing itself stand still,
  And in its image it transformed itself.

While with amazement filled and jubilant,
  My soul was tasting of the food, that while
  It satisfies us makes us hunger for it,

Themselves revealing of the highest rank
  In bearing, did the other three advance,
  Singing to their angelic saraband.

"Turn, Beatrice, O turn thy holy eyes,"
  Such was their song, "unto thy faithful one,
  Who has to see thee ta'en so many steps.

In grace do us the grace that thou unveil
  Thy face to him, so that he may discern
  The second beauty which thou dost conceal."

O splendor of the living light eternal!
  Who underneath the shadow of Parnassus
  Has grown so pale, or drunk so at its cistern,

He would not seem to have his mind encumbered
  Striving to paint thee as thou didst appear,
  Where the harmonious heaven o'ershadowed thee,

When in the open air thou didst unveil?

Canto XXXII

So steadfast and attentive were mine eyes
  In satisfying their decennial thirst,
  That all my other senses were extinct,

And upon this side and on that they had
  Walls of indifference, so the holy smile
  Drew them unto itself with the old net

When forcibly my sight was turned away
  Towards my left hand by those goddesses,
  Because I heard from them a "Too intently!"

And that condition of the sight which is
  In eyes but lately smitten by the sun
  Bereft me of my vision some short while;

But to the less when sight re-shaped itself,
  I say the less in reference to the greater
  Splendor from which perforce I had withdrawn,

I saw upon its right wing wheeled about
  The glorious host returning with the sun
  And with the sevenfold flames upon their faces.

As underneath its shields, to save itself,
  A squadron turns, and with its banner wheels,
  Before the whole thereof can change its front,

That soldiery of the celestial kingdom
  Which marched in the advance had wholly passed us
  Before the chariot had turned its pole.

Then to the wheels the maidens turned themselves,
  And the Griffin moved his burden benedight,
  But so that not a feather of him fluttered.

The lady fair who drew me through the ford
  Followed with Statius and myself the wheel
  Which made its orbit with the lesser arc.

So passing through the lofty forest, vacant
  By fault of her who in the serpent trusted,
  Angelic music made our steps keep time.

Perchance as great a space had in three flights
  An arrow loosened from the string o'erpassed,
  As we had moved when Beatrice descended.

I heard them murmur altogether, "Adam!"
  Then circled they about a tree despoiled
  Of blooms and other leafage on each bough.

Its tresses, which so much the more dilate
  As higher they ascend, had been by Indians
  Among their forests marvelled at for height.

"Blessed art thou, O Griffin, who dost not
  Pluck with thy beak these branches sweet to taste,
  Since appetite by this was turned to evil."

After this fashion round the tree robust
  The others shouted; and the twofold creature:
  "Thus is preserved the seed of all the just."

And turning to the pole which he had dragged,
  He drew it close beneath the widowed bough,
  And what was of it unto it left bound.

In the same manner as our trees (when downward
  Falls the great light, with that together mingled
  Which after the celestial Lasca shines)

Begin to swell, and then renew themselves,
  Each one with its own color, ere the Sun
  Harness his steeds beneath another star:

Less than of rose and more than violet
  A hue disclosing, was renewed the tree
  That had erewhile its boughs so desolate.

I never heard, nor here below is sung,
  The hymn which afterward that people sang,
  Nor did I bear the melody throughout.

Had I the power to paint how fell asleep
  Those eyes compassionless, of Syrinx hearing,
  Those eyes to which more watching cost so dear,

Even as a painter who from model paints
  I would portray how I was lulled asleep;
  He may, who well can picture drowsihood.

Therefore I pass to what time I awoke,
  And say a splendor rent from me the veil
  Of slumber, and a calling: "Rise, what dost thou?"

As to behold the apple-tree in blossom
  Which makes the Angels greedy for its fruit,
  And keeps perpetual bridals in the Heaven,

Peter and John and James conducted were,
  And, overcome, recovered at the word
  By which still greater slumbers have been broken,

And saw their school diminished by the loss
  Not only of Elias, but of Moses,
  And the apparel of their Master changed;

So I revived, and saw that piteous one
  Above me standing, who had been conductress
  Aforetime of my steps beside the river,

And all in doubt I said, "Where's Beatrice?"
  And she: "Behold her seated underneath
  The leafage new, upon the root of it.

Behold the company that circles her;
  The rest behind the Griffin are ascending
  With more melodious song, and more profound."

And if her speech were more diffuse I know not,
  Because already in my sight was she
  Who from the hearing of aught else had shut me.

Alone she sat upon the very earth,
  Left there as guardian of the chariot
  Which I had seen the biform monster fasten.

Encircling her, a cloister made themselves
  The seven Nymphs, with those lights in their hands
  Which are secure from Aquilon and Auster.

"Short while shalt thou be here a forester,
  And thou shalt be with me for evermore
  A citizen of that Rome where Christ is Roman.

Therefore, for that world's good which liveth ill,
  Fix on the car thine eyes, and what thou seest,
  Having returned to earth, take heed thou write."

Thus Beatrice; and I, who at the feet
  Of her commandments all devoted was,
  My mind and eyes directed where she willed.

Never descended with so swift a motion
  Fire from a heavy cloud, when it is raining
  From out the region which is most remote,

As I beheld the bird of Jove descend
  Down through the tree, rending away the bark,
  As well as blossoms and the foliage new,

And he with all his might the chariot smote,
  Whereat it reeled, like vessel in a tempest
  Tossed by the waves, now starboard and now larboard.

Thereafter saw I leap into the body
  Of the triumphal vehicle a Fox,
  That seemed unfed with any wholesome food.

But for his hideous sins upbraiding him,
  My Lady put him to as swift a flight
  As such a fleshless skeleton could bear.

Then by the way that it before had come,
  Into the chariot's chest I saw the Eagle
  Descend, and leave it feathered with his plumes.

And such as issues from a heart that mourns,
  A voice from Heaven there issued, and it said:
  "My little bark, how badly art thou freighted!"

Methought, then, that the earth did yawn between
  Both wheels, and I saw rise from it a Dragon,
  Who through the chariot upward fixed his tail,

And as a wasp that draweth back its sting,
  Drawing unto himself his tail malign,
  Drew out the floor, and went his way rejoicing.

That which remained behind, even as with grass
  A fertile region, with the feathers, offered
  Perhaps with pure intention and benign,

Reclothed itself, and with them were reclothed
  The pole and both the wheels so speedily,
  A sigh doth longer keep the lips apart.

Transfigured thus the holy edifice
  Thrust forward heads upon the parts of it,
  Three on the pole and one at either corner.

The first were horned like oxen; but the four
  Had but a single horn upon the forehead;
  A monster such had never yet been seen!

Firm as a rock upon a mountain high,
  Seated upon it, there appeared to me
  A shameless whore, with eyes swift glancing round,

And, as if not to have her taken from him,
  Upright beside her I beheld a giant;
  And ever and anon they kissed each other.

But because she her wanton, roving eye
  Turned upon me, her angry paramour
  Did scourge her from her head unto her feet.

Then full of jealousy, and fierce with wrath,
  He loosed the monster, and across the forest
  Dragged it so far, he made of that alone

A shield unto the whore and the strange beast.

Canto XXXIII

"Deus venerunt gentes," alternating
  Now three, now four, melodious psalmody
  The maidens in the midst of tears began;

And Beatrice, compassionate and sighing,
  Listened to them with such a countenance,
  That scarce more changed was Mary at the cross.

But when the other virgins place had given
  For her to speak, uprisen to her feet
  With color as of fire, she made response:

"'Modicum, et non videbitis me;
  Et iterum,' my sisters predilect,
  'Modicum, et vos videbitis me.'"

Then all the seven in front of her she placed;
  And after her, by beckoning only, moved
  Me and the lady and the sage who stayed.

So she moved onward; and I do not think
  That her tenth step was placed upon the ground,
  When with her eyes upon mine eyes she smote,

And with a tranquil aspect, "Come more quickly,"
  To me she said, "that, if I speak with thee,
  To listen to me thou mayst be well placed."

As soon as I was with her as I should be,
  She said to me: "Why, brother, dost thou not
  Venture to question now, in coming with me?"

As unto those who are too reverential,
  Speaking in presence of superiors,
  Who drag no living utterance to their teeth,

It me befell, that without perfect sound
  Began I: "My necessity, Madonna,
  You know, and that which thereunto is good."

And she to me: "Of fear and bashfulness
  Henceforward I will have thee strip thyself,
  So that thou speak no more as one who dreams.

Know that the vessel which the serpent broke
  Was, and is not; but let him who is guilty
  Think that God's vengeance does not fear a sop.

Without an heir shall not for ever be
  The Eagle that left his plumes upon the car,
  Whence it became a monster, then a prey;

For verily I see, and hence narrate it,
  The stars already near to bring the time,
  From every hindrance safe, and every bar,

Within which a Five-hundred, Ten, and Five,
  One sent from God, shall slay the thievish woman
  And that same giant who is sinning with her.

And peradventure my dark utterance,
  Like Themis and the Sphinx, may less persuade thee,
  Since, in their mode, it clouds the intellect;

But soon the facts shall be the Naiades
  Who shall this difficult enigma solve,
  Without destruction of the flocks and harvests.

Note thou; and even as by me are uttered
  These words, so teach them unto those who live
  That life which is a running unto death;

And bear in mind, whene'er thou writest them,
  Not to conceal what thou hast seen the plant,
  That twice already has been pillaged here.

Whoever pillages or shatters it,
  With blasphemy of deed offendeth God,
  Who made it holy for his use alone.

For biting that, in pain and in desire
Five thousand years and more the first-born soul
Craved Him, who punished in himself the bite.

Thy genius slumbers, if it deem it not
For special reason so pre-eminent
In height, and so inverted in its summit.

And if thy vain imaginings had not been
Water of Elsa round about thy mind,
And Pyramus to the mulberry, their pleasure,

Thou by so many circumstances only
The justice of the interdict of God
Morally in the tree wouldst recognize.

But since I see thee in thine intellect
Converted into stone and stained with sin,
So that the light of my discourse doth daze thee,

I will too, if not written, at least painted,
Thou bear it back within thee, for the reason
That cinct with palm the pilgrim's staff is borne."

And I: "As by a signet is the wax
Which does not change the figure stamped upon it,
My brain is now imprinted by yourself.

But wherefore so beyond my power of sight
Soars your desirable discourse, that aye
The more I strive, so much the more I lose it?"

"That thou mayst recognize," she said, "the school
Which thou hast followed, and mayst see how far
Its doctrine follows after my discourse,

And mayst behold your path from the divine
Distant as far as separated is
From earth the heaven that highest hastens on."

Whence her I answered: "I do not remember
That ever I estranged myself from you,
Nor have I conscience of it that reproves me."

"And if thou art not able to remember,"
  Smiling she answered, "recollect thee now
  That thou this very day hast drunk of Lethe;

And if from smoke a fire may be inferred,
  Such an oblivion clearly demonstrates
  Some error in thy will elsewhere intent.

Truly from this time forward shall my words
  Be naked, so far as it is befitting
  To lay them open unto thy rude gaze."

And more coruscant and with slower steps
  The sun was holding the meridian circle,
  Which, with the point of view, shifts here and there

When halted (as he cometh to a halt,
  Who goes before a squadron as its escort,
  If something new he find upon his way)

The ladies seven at a dark shadow's edge,
  Such as, beneath green leaves and branches black,
  The Alp upon its frigid border wears.

In front of them the Tigris and Euphrates
  Methought I saw forth issue from one fountain,
  And slowly part, like friends, from one another.

"O light, O glory of the human race!
  What stream is this which here unfolds itself
  From out one source, and from itself withdraws?"

For such a prayer, 'twas said unto me, "Pray
  Matilda that she tell thee;" and here answered,
  As one does who doth free himself from blame,

The beautiful lady: "This and other things
  Were told to him by me; and sure I am
  The water of Lethe has not hid them from him."

And Beatrice: "Perhaps a greater care,
  Which oftentimes our memory takes away,
  Has made the vision of his mind obscure.

But Eunoe behold, that yonder rises;
  Lead him to it, and, as thou art accustomed,
  Revive again the half-dead virtue in him."

Like gentle soul, that maketh no excuse,
  But makes its own will of another's will
  As soon as by a sign it is disclosed,

Even so, when she had taken hold of me,
  The beautiful lady moved, and unto Statius
  Said, in her womanly manner, "Come with him."

If, Reader, I possessed a longer space
  For writing it, I yet would sing in part
  Of the sweet draught that ne'er would satiate me;

But inasmuch as full are all the leaves
  Made ready for this second canticle,
  The curb of art no farther lets me go.

From the most holy water I returned
  Regenerate, in the manner of new trees
  That are renewed with a new foliage,

Pure and disposed to mount unto the stars.

THE END

www.ingramcontent.com/pod-product-compliance
Lightning Source LLC
Chambersburg PA
CBHW022132170626
46808CB00002B/955